"Megan. Gently lower the painting to the floor and back away."

"Back away?" she repeated, her voice reedy.

He took her by the shoulders. "Lower the painting."

Slowly, she let it fall, and the painting came to a rest on the floor of her closet. She stepped back, allowing him to propel her toward the front door. He captured her outstretched hand before she could touch the knob.

"We've contaminated the scene enough," he said, and pulled out a pair of rubber gloves. He slipped one on and opened the door.

When they cleared the threshold, he used his cell phone to call dispatch.

Megan looked so small and vulnerable. He resisted the urge to take her in his arms. He had to stay objective. "We'll wait for the CSI team."

"And then?"

Regret lay heavy across his shoulders. "Then I have to take you in."

Books by Terri Reed

Love Inspired Suspense

Strictly Confidential
*Double Deception
Beloved Enemy
Her Christmas Protector
*Double Jeopardy
*Double Cross
*Double Threat Christmas

*The McClains

Love Inspired

Love Comes Home
A Sheltering Love
A Sheltering Heart
A Time of Hope
Giving Thanks for Baby

TERRI REED

At an early age Terri Reed discovered the wonderful world of fiction and declared she would one day write a book. Now she is fulfilling that dream and enjoys writing for Steeple Hill Books. Her second book, *A Sheltering Love,* was a 2006 RITA® Award Finalist and a 2005 National Readers' Choice Award Finalist. Her book *Strictly Confidential,* book five of the Faith at the Crossroads continuity series, took third place in the 2007 American Christian Fiction Writers Book of the Year Award. She is an active member of both Romance Writers of America and American Christian Fiction Writers. She resides in the Pacific Northwest with her college-sweetheart husband, two wonderful children and an array of critters. When not writing, she enjoys spending time with her family and friends, gardening and playing with her dogs.

You can write to Terri at P.O. Box 19555, Portland, OR 97280, visit her on the Web at www.loveinspiredauthors.com, or leave comments on her blog at http://ladiesofsuspense.blogspot.com/.

Terri Reed

DOUBLE THREAT

Christmas

Steeple
Hill®

Published by Steeple Hill Books™

STEEPLE HILL BOOKS

Steeple
Hill®

ISBN-13: 978-0-373-44317-8
ISBN-10:   0-373-44317-X

DOUBLE THREAT CHRISTMAS

www.SteepleHill.com

Printed in U.S.A.

Every good thing bestowed and every perfect gift
is from above, coming down from the Father of
lights, with whom there is no variation,
or shifting shadows.

—*James* 1:17

To my family, for putting up with the long hours at the keyboard. I love you all.

ONE

"I didn't kill those men!"

The declaration so angrily delivered by the petite curator of New York City's Sinclair Art Gallery held more sincerity than most perps'.

Even so, homicide detective Paul Wallace barely managed to contain his scoff. He'd heard those exact words way too many times during the course of his law-enforcement career.

And denial was the fallback in every situation for most suspects.

Even suspects as lovely as Megan McClain.

Upscale all the way in her well-fitting, short-sleeved red dress and intricately patterned black pumps. Not exactly attire suited for the December snowstorm raging outside. She probably had a change of clothes stashed for the trek home—a planner.

Paul gauged her height at five feet five without the two-inch heels. She was about a hundred and ten pounds of slopes and angles. Raven-black hair fell past her shoulders, and her vivid blue eyes, the pupils dilated slightly, were set symmetrically within her pale, heart-shaped face.

The rapid beat of her heart was evident at the carotid pulse point on her graceful neck. Was she experiencing shock or remorse?

Paul glanced around, quickly assessing and cataloging the crime scene. Beyond the faintest trace of spent gunpowder and the coppery odor of blood, he detected a citruslike scent. On the yellow walls of the room they stood in, painted works of art were hung, and little display lights threw a glow on the framed pieces, creating a half circle of light on the floor beneath the bodies.

He noted that across the top threshold of each doorway, leading to other rooms full of artwork, a black seam hid a gate that would drop down if the security system was activated. Those gates were up. No alarm had been sounded. High in the corner of the room was a security monitor.

Pulling his focus back to Ms. McClain, he shrugged out of his overcoat and laid it across the crook of one arm.

"Did you hear me, Detective…?" she demanded, all spitfire and ready to explode. "Why would I call 911 if I'd killed them?"

Paul ignored her question as irrelevant, because too often the perpetrator of a crime was also the one to call 911 in an attempt to deflect the police from looking too closely at themselves. He would consider Megan McClain a suspect/potential witness, until he knew more.

"Detective Wallace," he supplied, and flipped open his notebook to reread what he'd already learned from the responding officer. "You were read your Miranda rights. Do you fully understand these rights?"

She waved an impatient hand. "Yes, of course."

"Good. So you were working here alone. Is that correct?"

"Yes. I mean no. I thought my boss was upstairs. I already went through all this with the other officer," she huffed, and pushed a lock of hair back behind her ear to reveal sparkling stones. "And then again with those other people who practically strip-searched me." A shudder rippled over her.

The CSI team had performed a routine exam of her person for trace evidence, checking her hands for gunpowder residue, taking any out-of-place fibers off her clothing and looking for blood droplets that would match the victims. The team had done their job.

Now it was his turn. Interviewing the suspects and witnesses was a vital aspect of any investigation, especially done as closely to the crime as possible while the person's memory was fresh and they hadn't had time to embellish or minimize any details.

"I understand that, ma'am. Nevertheless, I need you to go through it again with me," Paul explained.

He'd look for inconsistencies in her account of the events and for ways to dig deeper and sift truth from lies.

She blinked her long lashes. "Fine. My assistant had an appointment, so she'd left early. I was alone in the workroom preparing the Wahlberer painting for transport when Mr. Drake—" She gestured to one of the two dead men lying on the floor to the right.

Ms. McClain seemed momentarily frozen as she stared at the dark-haired man sprawled on the shining cherrywood floor. A pair of long-handled sheers protruded from the man's gut, and blood spilled out to stain the floor a deep crimson. The click and flash of the CSI tech's camera documenting the death echoed in the room along with the hushed whispers of those working the scene.

A stabbing indicated a crime of passion.

"Mr. Drake came in…" Paul prompted, wondering if there was enough fire in her blood to make her commit murder.

She turned sharply back to him, visibly refocusing, her breathing a bit irregular. "Mr. Drake arrived early. He wasn't due for another fifteen minutes. I wasn't ready. I asked him to wait in the red room."

Paul arched an eyebrow. "The red room?"

She made a sweeping gesture with one elegant hand toward the doorways. "The different art collections are housed in separate rooms. Each room is color-coded."

"I see. So Mr. Drake went into the red room."

"No." She pointed to the other vic lying a few feet away. "He—Mr. Vanderpool—stormed in even before Mr. Drake had taken five steps."

Vanderpool was as Nordic as they came with his white-blond hair and large features. His wounds were consistent with a gunshot wound. But they wouldn't know for certain until the medical examiner did the autopsy.

"You say he stormed in? Why do you say it like that?" Paul watched her closely, gauging her response.

Would her gaze dart upward and to the right, searching for a fabrication, or would her eyes go up and to the left, recalling events and words of description?

She stared straight at him with those eerily blue, sharply intelligent eyes, no shifting, no blinking. "Mr. Vanderpool and Mr. Drake both wanted the Wahlberer painting. At the auction last night both men created quite a stir when they tried to outbid each other. Mr. Vanderpool stormed in claiming the painting was supposed to be his."

She gave a look that spoke volumes of how dumbfounded she was by the men's behavior. "I thought it strange that either would find the painting that valuable since Wahlberer is so new to the art world." She gave a delicate shrug of her slim shoulders. "People who are passionate about art are an eclectic breed."

Paul wouldn't know since he wasn't much interested in art. His focus was on contributing to society by getting the job done and putting away the bad guys. "And where is this Wahlberer now?"

The painting had not been found in the workroom as she'd claimed it should be.

Her mouth pressed into a thin line. "I don't know.

I last saw it in the workroom on the table, wrapped in brown packaging. I hadn't yet put the string across to secure it before I was interrupted."

"By Mr. Drake?"

"Yes. By Mr. Drake." Frustration clearly marked her words.

"What was your relationship with Mr. Drake?"

She stared at him aghast. "There was no relationship. He bought art through the gallery. That's it."

Her denial rang true. "How much is the painting worth?"

"Mr. Drake bought the painting for a hundred thousand dollars."

Ah. Motivation enough for someone to kill and steal. Even an art curator. He made a note to check into Megan's finances. "Who knew that Mr. Drake was coming to pick up the painting?"

"The staff. But none of them would do this," she protested, her lip quivering.

That remained to be seen. "You left the painting on the table."

"Yes."

He noticed she didn't fidget or hedge.

When she remained silent he pressed, "And then?"

"I went to find my boss, Lester Sinclair. I thought he was in his office upstairs. But he wasn't."

"Did you knock or just go in?" He'd have the CSI team check out the second floor and hall for any trace evidence.

She folded her hands together in front of her. He

noted her nails were short and her skin red and dry. As if she'd scrubbed at them. Possibly washing away blood? He made a note of his observation on his notepad.

"I knocked first and then I went in. His office was empty," she stated, her voice curiously flat.

"Is there a back way from the offices upstairs to the gallery floor?"

Two little lines appeared between her black arched eyebrows. "Yes. There's another staircase that leads to the back of the gallery, near the restrooms." Horror filled her expression. "But you can't think Mr. Sinclair could have done this. He's nearly seventy years old. Why would he commit such a heinous crime?" She tugged her bottom lip between her white, straight teeth.

He arched his eyebrow. "If you're sure he wasn't in the building, then why'd you go looking for him?"

"I didn't know he wasn't in the building at the time," she replied, her eyes widening, expressing her agitation. "Only now I know."

"And you didn't hear anything?"

"I heard the gunshots." She blinked rapidly as if to hold back tears. "I ran back downstairs and found them. My scissors were in Mr. Drake's stomach." She shuddered.

Practiced at not being moved by displays of emotion, he consulted his notes again. "Gunshots? As in more than one?"

She nodded with certainty. "Yes. Two."

He made a note to tell the crime-scene techs to look for a stray bullet since they had only one GSW. "And your assistant, Lacy Knight, had an appointment. Where?"

She shook her head; her dark hair swayed slightly. "I don't know. I don't keep tabs on her or the other employees."

"How many employees were here today and when did they leave?" he probed.

Without hesitation, she answered, "Joanie, the receptionist, left at five as always. Donny and George are the daytime security guards. They both left at six."

The call came in to 911 at five minutes to seven. "There was no night-shift guard?"

"Usually there is." She frowned, her pert little nose crinkling slightly. "But Mack didn't show. Lacy said he called in sick. Mr. Sinclair was going to get a temp from the security company we use but I didn't hear what happened with that."

"We'll need the names and numbers for all the employees."

"You'll have to talk to Mr. Sinclair," she stated as her gaze fixated on the men from the coroner's office as they began to remove the two bodies from the gallery floor.

Paul positioned himself in her line of vision. He wanted to keep her focused. "Is there an exit through the workroom to the outside?"

Giving herself a little shake, she shifted her bright

blue gaze to him. "Yes. But it's locked. If anyone had come in or out, the alarm would have gone off. And the security camera would record it."

"We'll need the video feed on the camera from the time of the murders," Paul said.

"You'll have to talk to Mr. Sinclair about that."

"Hey, Wallace," Andy Howell, Paul's partner for the past six months, called from the doorway to the workroom. He'd also taken off his overcoat to reveal his navy suit, one most detectives couldn't afford, but Andy's wife owned a clothing shop and liked her husband to dress well.

More than six feet tall, Andy had once been a college basketball player until he blew out a knee. He still had a slight limp, but Paul wouldn't trust his back to anyone else. In the short time they'd been partnered, Paul had come to admire and respect Andy.

"We found the other murder weapon," Andy stated as he approached.

Paul's gaze jumped to Megan to see her reaction. She showed no effects of Andy's announcement. Innocence? Or confidence?

Paul nodded to a uniformed officer standing close by. "Take Ms. McClain to the station."

Her blue eyes widened with panic, her body stiffened, her arms straight and held tight against her sides, her knees and feet pressed together. "You want me to go to the station."

"Yes," he replied, forcing patience into his tone.

That's usually what happened to murder suspects, but he refrained from pointing that out. "We'll need a formal statement."

"How?"

He frowned. "How what?"

She seemed to have trouble finding her voice. "How…how are we going to the station?"

"By car. I certainly don't plan on making you walk ten blocks in a snowstorm." His trousers were still damp from when he'd walked the short distance from the car to the gallery entrance.

"Car," she repeated. "Cars are safe."

His curiosity piqued by her odd behavior, Paul said, "Officer Johnson will escort you to find your coat and then he'll take you to the station. I'll see you again there."

"Can I change? My shoes at least?" she asked, her expression nearing panic.

Paul hid a smile at having pegged her correctly and sought for a soothing tone. "Of course you may."

She moved stiffly to a panel of wall behind the reception desk. With a little push the panel opened, revealing a closet.

Paul exchanged a curious glance with his partner.

"I'll tell Sims," Andy stated and retreated back to the workroom to inform the lead CSI of the secret hole in the wall.

Megan retrieved a pair of tall, black snow boots. Methodically, she unzipped each boot then grabbed an aerosol can from a shelf inside the closet and sprayed the insides of each one. The scent of lemon filled the air.

Then Megan slipped one foot out of a pump, while balancing on the other heeled shoe while she carefully placed her stocking foot into the boot. She repeated the process with the other foot then bent to zip up each boot.

Figuring she was done, Paul started to turn away, but stopped to watch in rapt fascination as she once again reached for something on the shelf inside the closet. This time she pulled out a moist square sheet, which she used to thoroughly wipe each pump down before putting the shoes in the closet where the boots once had been.

Then using the same moistened wipe, she ran the cloth over the door panel where she'd touched the wall before pressing the wood back into place. Using the tips of two fingers, she dropped the cloth into the wastebasket.

With a tenuous smile, she announced to Officer Johnson, "I'm ready."

That was some routine. The woman became more interesting each passing second. And by the time he was done he'd get to know her a whole lot better.

Paul noted the stiff way she held herself as Johnson helped her don her long woolen coat. Johnson took her elbow to lead her out and she shied away. Like someone once abused? Or did she just not like being touched?

The officer shrugged, dropped his hand and

opened the gallery's front door for her to pass through. At the last moment, before stepping outside, she turned her head and met Paul's gaze.

There was panic in her eyes. Fear, maybe. But also something else, something vulnerable, that slammed into his gut.

Hating that he'd let his guard slip even a fraction, Paul shook himself and dispensed with any softening toward Ms. McClain.

Obviously, if he saw fear in her eyes it was only because she was guilty.

Fifty-two steps.

That's how many footsteps Megan counted as she was led to the waiting police vehicle at the curb. She shivered as flakes of snow covered her hair and landed on her face. Her heart thudded in her chest, making breathing difficult. Horror nearly choked her. She fought for control, but any semblance of control had been taken away from her.

By a murderer.

Two men had been killed, and she was the number one suspect.

With a father who had been a cop on the Boston police force and a brother who was a sheriff, she knew the law would shield her. The maxim "innocent until proven guilty" would hold, but it wouldn't save her from accusations and assumptions. Her only real protection would come from God.

Just as her psychologist, Dr. Miller, had suggested

she do when she was confronted by any source of fear, she whispered the mantra over and over, "When I'm afraid, I'll trust in the Lord. When I'm afraid, I'll trust in the Lord."

She took comfort in her faith even as disbelief and terror that this whole nightmare was happening took hold of her stomach and twisted her insides into tight knots.

Officer Johnson, twentysomething with a clean-shaven jaw and a lump at the bridge of his nose, opened the back door of the white cruiser with the blue lettering of the NYPD across the side.

Her gaze strayed to the ten-story building a half a block away. She counted the windows up three floors and across six to her apartment. She just wanted to go home and cocoon herself inside the four walls where everything was neat and orderly. Where there were no dead men, and no police detective who looked at her with accusation in his jade-colored eyes, making her feel like she were scum on the bottom of his shoe.

"Ma'am," Officer Johnson prodded with a gesture to the interior of the car.

Swallowing back her panic, she told herself, *Cars are safe.* She'd be safe. Nothing bad was going to happen to her in the car. Only in a car she wasn't in control. Walking, she could control. She could control her steps, her pace and her path.

She slid onto the seat in the back of the cruiser, the cracked leather creaking beneath her. The car smelled like stale coffee and greasy food, making her stomach riot with nausea. She shuddered, wishing she had her lemon-scented air freshener handy.

Officer Johnson slid into the driver's seat and soon they were sloshing their way through the late evening traffic.

She stared straight ahead and briefly met the officer's gaze in the rearview mirror. Did he, too, think she killed those men?

Quickly she averted her eyes to watch the neighborhood go by. She counted how many people she saw wearing brimmed hats, beanie caps and how many were braving the elements with bare heads. But she kept losing count as the frightening picture of the two dead men crept into her mind.

The image of her scissors embedded deep into the stomach of Mr. Drake would forever be imprinted on her brain.

She gagged, fighting to control her body's need to lose the salad she'd had for dinner.

She replayed the whole evening over and over again, looking for some way to make the outcome different. But that was an impossibility.

The past could not be undone.

A lesson she'd learned long ago but still struggled to come to terms with. She so wanted to be able to turn the clock back, to force events to be redone so that her father wouldn't have been murdered and her life shattered by grief and illness.

Stop it, she commanded herself. She wouldn't go

down that road. Not now. Now, she had to think about tonight and the two men who had died in the gallery.

She'd been in the workroom tending to the Wahlberer, a lovely landscape of the Mexican Riviera, with lots of color and bold strokes that were softened by featherlight shading that inspired, giving the onlooker a sense of place that only the masters usually accomplished.

But she'd met the artist Wahlberer, a talented young upstart out of Canada who'd flirted shamelessly and hadn't really taken seriously his good fortune at having his work displayed at the Sinclair Gallery. His flippant attitude about his art and the gallery had grated on her nerves.

As she'd told Detective Wallace, she couldn't understand the compulsion of either of the two dead men to buy the painting. The amount had been way above the value, and, yes, a boon for the gallery and the artist, but a poor investment in her mind.

Then when Mr. Vanderpool had shown up, saying he'd been told that he could have the painting, the yelling had started. Overwhelmed by the feral angriness of the two men, Megan had retreated in search of her boss.

Why hadn't Sinclair been in his office? He always worked until eight. A shiver hit her flesh as possibilities of what could have happened ran rampant through her brain.

There had been another person in the gallery. But who? And why murder the two men?

A thought clamped on to her mind and wouldn't let go. If she hadn't gone in search of her boss, would she, too, have been killed?

TWO

"A 9 mm revolver," Andy said, holding up the weapon with his pencil through the trigger guard. "Found in the Dumpster out back."

Paul moved to the exit leading to the back alley of the building. Putting his overcoat back on before stepping outside, he blinked to clear his vision as a sheet of cold snow hit him in the face. A streetlamp provided a small measure of light over the Dumpsters, while lamps had been set up to illuminate the work area for the CSI team as they continued their part of the investigation.

Paul found the team leader and asked her to extend the search in the upper part of gallery.

"Already on it," Barbara Sims stated in her no-nonsense way. "We've dusted the door and lifted at least a dozen prints on the outside, but inside, *every-thing...*" She paused to emphasize her words. "And I mean nearly every square inch of that workroom has been wiped clean."

Megan rubbing down her pumps before using the

cloth to set them on the floor of the closet flashed in Paul's mind.

Had her routine with the shoes been for real or for show?

He reentered the workroom, his gaze taking in the orderly way the room was arranged. Packing materials lined up neatly in one corner, brushes hung upside down from a rack, shortest to longest. The worktable where Megan claimed to have been working hardly looked messy at all.

A ball of string sat on one corner of the table, a tape dispenser beside it, a ruler next and a roll of brown packing paper, all lined up with the beveled edge. Everything one would need to secure a package, except the scissors.

"Lemon," Paul said as he breathed in the scent.

Andy held up a can of lemon-scented air freshener. One of five that were lined along the bottom shelf of the workbench. "This."

The same spray Megan had used earlier. Paul also noted the dozen boxes of antibacterial wipes stacked next to the air-freshener cans.

A commotion back in the gallery drew Paul's attention. He and Andy moved together out of the workroom and found a uniformed officer trying to prevent a short, thin, elderly gentlemen, wearing a long trench coat, from entering the crime scene.

"What's going on here?" the man asked, his nasally voice echoing off the walls. "I'm Lester Sinclair. I own this gallery." Mr. Sinclair spotted Paul and directed his words to him. "I demand you tell me what's going on this instant."

Paul nodded for the officer to let Mr. Sinclair pass. "Sir, I'm Detective Wallace and this is my partner, Detective Howell. There has been a double homicide on the premises."

Mr. Sinclair's face turned ashen. "Oh, mercy no. Is Megan…?"

"Ms. McClain is fine. She's been taken to the station for further questioning." Paul pulled out his notepad. Keeping meticulous records of all interviews had served him well over the years, especially when some ambitious defense attorney tried to reinvent testimony.

"Who's been killed?" Sinclair rose on the toes of his brown loafers, trying to look past Paul's shoulder.

"A Thomas Drake and a Henry Vanderpool. Do you know them?"

Recognition registered in Sinclair's green eyes. "What was Mr. Vanderpool doing here? He lost the bid on the painting last night."

"That's a good question." So that confirmed what Megan had said about Vanderpool not being expected, only Drake. "Where have you been for the past three hours?"

Sinclair's eyes widened. "I was here, until 6:00 p.m. Then I went out to get a bite to eat since I skipped lunch."

"And where did you dine tonight?" Andy asked.

Sinclair cast him an irritated glance. "What does it matter?"

Andy leaned in intimidatingly closer. "Establishes an alibi."

Sinclair blanched. "Oh. Oh, well, I was at Figaro's."

Paul arched an eyebrow at the name of the well-known restaurant where reservations were required to be made at least a month in advance. And Sinclair just decided to pop in for dinner? "Did you inform your curator that you were leaving?"

Sinclair frowned. "I don't answer to my staff."

Almost the same statement that Megan had made. "What about a night-shift security guard?" Paul questioned.

"Mack called in sick. It's the third time this week. I think I'm going to have to fire him. The security company we use was supposed to send someone over at five. I assumed since Megan hadn't said anything to the contrary that the guard had arrived as scheduled."

Interesting. Megan claimed she didn't know what was happening with the security guards. "So you informed Ms. McClain that a replacement guard would be arriving at five."

"Yes." He paused for a moment, a thoughtful look crossing his thin face. "Or maybe I just told Lacy." He shook his head, his gaze befuddled. "I don't really recall. Oh, what a mess. This will be bad for business." He grabbed Andy's arm. "Can you keep this out of the paper?"

"Doubtful, once the pariah of the media get a whiff of murder," Andy stated with contempt and shook off Sinclair's hand.

"The assistant who'd left early for an appointment?" Paul asked to keep the focus on the investigation. He wasn't concerned with Sinclair's business or reputation.

Sinclair sighed. "Yes. She's always running off to one appointment or another."

Convenience or coincidence? Paul would find out. "I'm going to need the names and addresses of all your employees and anyone else who has the security codes for the gallery."

"Yes, of course. You can have anything you want," Sinclair said, and pointed up with his long, bony finger. "All that information is in my office."

"We'll also need the video feed from the monitors in the yellow room and if there's one in the workroom," Paul stated.

Sinclair grimaced. "Actually, the video monitors are deterrents only. Our security is set up to stop theft, not catch a murderer. All the pieces of art are wired so if they are removed or tampered with, the gates go down."

Frustration beat a steady tattoo at Paul's temple. Video of the murders would have been so much more efficient in apprehending the villain.

Paul escorted Sinclair upstairs, and after getting a nod to go ahead from the CSI techs, they entered the plush, opulent office. A wall of windows overlooked Lexington Avenue. Paul made a note to check the building across the street and find anyone who might have seen something at the gallery.

Sinclair went to his glass-topped desk and fired up his notebook computer. "Everything is computerized these days," he said as he hit some keys. The printer on the glass sidebar started to hum and spit out papers.

"How would you describe Megan McClain?" Paul asked.

Sinclair's chin rose and pride entered his voice. "She is an exemplary employee. Trustworthy, hard-working and…and very organized."

"And Lacy Knight?"

"Ah, Lacy." His chin dropped and his voice softened. "Young, a bit flighty but she tries. She's my great-niece, you know. Some day she'll make a good curator," Sinclair replied as he gathered the papers from the printer and handed them to Paul.

Taking the printed sheets with the employee records, Paul met his partner at the front door.

"I've sent some uniforms to canvass the neighborhood," Andy informed Paul.

"Good." Paul headed toward the entrance. "We need to find the assistant, Lacy. I have some questions for her."

"Detectives," called Sims from the doorway of the women's restroom. "There are traces of blood in the sink and drain."

Megan's raw, red hands popped into Paul's mind. "Get back to me on any DNA you find besides the vics'."

Sims inclined her head in acknowledgment and went back to work.

Andy shook his head. "I think what happened was McClain hadn't wanted to give up the painting. She gutted Drake but didn't expect Vanderpool to show up, so she used the gun on him. Now instead of just one body to deal with she had two. So she calls 911 and makes up the story about going to find her boss."

For some reason the whole scenario bummed Paul out.

Megan McClain had definitely become a full-fledged suspect.

"Wallace. Howell." A man just entering the building called to the detectives.

Paul glanced at Andy and saw the same surprise reflected in Andy's dark eyes that was shooting through Paul. What was Chief Erickson doing here?

"Chief," Andy said to the older, balding man.

Chief Erickson shook the snow off his hat as he moved closer. "I heard about our double homicide. I know the victims."

"I'm sorry," Paul said, sympathy coating his words.

Erickson's brown eyes revealed sadness. "Me, too. So tell me what you have."

Paul filled the chief in on their suspect Megan and explained what little evidence had been gathered so far. "After we inform the families, we'll check out the alibi for the owner and find out where the other employees were at the time of the murders."

"I'll inform the families," the chief said, his voice gruff.

A jolt of relief sparked through Paul. Telling the

victims' families of their loved ones' death was never pleasant.

"You want one of us to go with you?" Andy asked, compassion evident in his voice.

The chief shook his head. "I'll take Gonzales and a uniform with me. I think I'll call Shelia Wells, as well."

Paul thought having a crisis counselor on hand when delivering the heartbreaking news a brilliant idea. And taking Detective Maria Gonzales was also another smart move. Maria's ability to calm people and at the same time gain information was legendary within the department. The chief knew what he was doing when he called Maria. Paul respected the man and looked forward to many years of tutelage under his command.

"We'll go do our interviews," Andy said, and headed toward the door.

Paul followed Andy out the gallery entrance and into the deluge of snow; within seconds Paul's hair was soaked. They hustled into their unmarked sedan, Andy at the wheel.

"So what do you think?" Andy questioned as he maneuvered the car around some pedestrians hurrying across the street, their heads tucked low.

"It doesn't look good for Ms. McClain," Paul stated.

Means, motive and opportunity.

But a niggling of doubt lifted the hairs at Paul's nape. Somehow he couldn't see Megan, who exercised extreme sanitary measures, leaving behind such a bloody mess.

* * *

The phone rang. Once, twice. Then was answered on the third ring. "Hello?"

"It's done," the caller said with a slight tremor.

Silence met the announcement, followed closely by a sigh. One of relief or regret, the caller didn't know. And didn't care. This was about money, not emotion.

"Thank you."

"I didn't do this for your gratitude. And I want double the money since it was double the trouble," the caller stated in harsh tones.

"What? What do you mean double? I am not paying you more than what we agreed on."

"Oh, yes, you are." The caller's voice took on an edge of steel. "Because I'm not going away. If you think I haven't taken steps to protect myself on this, you'd be wrong."

A strangled sound came over the line. "I'll get you the money."

"I know." The caller hung up.

"Let's follow up on Sinclair's alibi. There's something about the guy that sets my teeth on edge," Paul said, thinking how convenient it was that the owner would leave early just in time for the murders to take place.

Within a few minutes, they'd made the trek to Figaro's. The savory smells of spices filled Paul's senses, making his stomach rumble. The clinking of expensive dinnerware and hushed voices could be heard over the soft classical music playing in the background. Paul's gaze swept over the mirrored walls, plush seating and white, linen tablecloths where the powerful came to do business and be seen.

A long, oak bar with high stools and brass appointments ran the length of the restaurant. Men in business suits and women in high-fashion styles nursed drinks while assumedly waiting for an available table.

Paul and Andy flashed their badges to the hostess, a pretty woman in her late twenties with long, straight, red hair, which covered her shoulders and made a stark contrast to the silky green shift she wore.

She blinked, her gaze shifting from Andy to Paul and back.

Andy gestured to Paul. "We have a few questions."

The young woman beamed and thrust out her ample chest. "Sure, anything for you. I'm Gina."

"Gina, do you remember a Mr. Lester Sinclair coming in earlier this evening?" Paul asked. "Short, thin, sixties?"

Her head bobbed. "The art guy, sure. He's a regular."

Paul pulled out his notepad. An expensive habit. "What time did he come in tonight?"

Gina thought for a moment. "He came in at about six something. He wanted to sit in Angela's section, so he had to wait for a bit."

"Why did he want Angela?" Paul inquired.

Gina's smile turned sly. "She's more his speed."

"Can we speak with Angela?" Andy asked.

"Let me get her," Gina replied, and sashayed away.

A moment later, Gina returned, followed by a tall, regal-looking older woman dressed in black slacks and blouse with a white apron.

Judging by the lines at the corners of her eyes and mouth, Paul put her at fifty-five-ish, but her figure belied her age. Her dark hair had been swept back into a sleek twist, and the woman exuded a graceful elegance that was indicative of Figaro's.

"Gentlemen, can I help you?" Angela's throaty voice held just a hint of mild curiosity.

"We'd like to ask you a few questions about Mr. Sinclair," Andy stated.

Angela inclined her head. "Ask away."

"We understand that Mr. Sinclair was here this evening, is that correct?" Paul asked.

A coy smile played at her red lips. "Yes. He came in and, as usual, waited to be seated in my section. He had the house specialty. Then he moved to the bar for a cocktail."

"So he *is* a regular?" Paul asked.

"Yes. Twice a week for the past, oh, gosh, five years."

"So you know him pretty well?" Andy asked.

She gave him a haughty stare. "Yes. I like to get to know my customers."

"When would you say he left the restaurant?" Paul inquired, drawing her attention.

"I really couldn't say. He sat at the bar for a while." Angela gestured to the bar. "You should ask Rod."

"We will," Andy said, and moved to the bar.

"Thank you for your time," Paul said. "Just one last question. Does Sinclair normally come in on Tuesday nights?"

Angela's eyebrows drew together. "Now that you mention it, no. Usually Thursday nights and Friday afternoons for lunch. I often sit with him for a while on Thursday nights. But tonight we were slammed, so I wasn't able to."

Paul narrowed his gaze. "Do you usually sit with your customers?"

She gave him a bold smile. "Only the ones that tip well."

"Ah. Thank you. If I have any other questions, I'll know where to find you." Paul joined Andy with the bartender, Rod.

"Rod, here, was just saying that Sinclair joined a young woman at the bar tonight," Andy informed Paul.

Paul recorded the information in his notepad. "Did you happen to hear the woman's name?"

Rod, a muscular man with a crew cut and a scar on one cheek, shook his head. "No, sorry, dude. She came in and sat here nursing a glass of house wine. When Sinclair got up to leave, she halted him and invited him to sit with her. I got the impression he was surprised. They both drank a scotch and sat talking for about forty minutes, maybe longer. I was busy, so I didn't hear any of their conversation."

"What time did he leave?" Paul asked.

"Eight-ish, I think."

Paul exchanged a glance with Andy. So far Sinclair's alibi checked out. "Was he here the whole time?"

Rod shrugged. "I don't know what time he came in. He ordered his first drink from me sometime after seven."

"Did the woman pay with a credit card?" Andy asked.

Rod shook his head. "No. Actually, Mr. Sinclair picked up the tab."

"For her wine, as well?" Paul asked.

"Yeah."

"Can you describe her?" Andy asked.

Rod raised his hand shoulder height. "She was about so tall, curvy in the right places. Blond, blue-eyed. Pretty."

Paul gauged Rod to be about six feet. If the woman came only to his shoulder, she was about five-five or -six. "Had you seen her before?"

"No. First time on my shift. But I could tell she wasn't comfortable here. A couple of guys tried hitting on her, but she made it clear she wasn't interested."

Paul exchanged a curious glance with Andy.

Paul closed his notebook. "You've been a big help."

Andy handed the guy a card. "If you think of anything else about Sinclair or the lady, let us know."

Rod slipped the card into the pocket of his black silk dress shirt. "Yeah, sure."

"Just a sec," Paul said to Andy. "I have one last question for Angela."

He tracked her down near the kitchen doors.

She paused with a plate of salad greens in hand and a pepper grinder tucked against her body by her elbow. "Detective? Was there something else?"

"One last question. Did Sinclair stay in his seat the whole time he was in your section?"

She thought for a moment. "No. He actually was gone for about ten minutes. I assume he used the facilities."

Time unaccounted for. Paul jotted that down. "Thanks."

Paul preceded Andy out of the restaurant and to the car. He shook off the snow and climbed in. Once they were moving, Paul said, "Alibi has some holes. And he changed his pattern. Angela said he usually comes in on Thursdays for dinner and Fridays for lunch. Why'd he go to Figaro's tonight, exactly when the murders were taking place? And she said he left his table for a while. The gallery's not that far from here. He could have slipped out the back and gone to the gallery, killed Drake and Vanderpool and then returned without anyone questioning him."

"Yeah. Could have happened like that. He must be one quick clean-up artist though," Andy stated dryly. "What's with the woman? Random or what?"

"I don't know. But it's interesting that Sinclair didn't mention the lady. Probably more worried about his wife finding out." Paul consulted the papers with the employees' addresses on it that he'd received from Sinclair. "Let's go see the assistant."

Paul gave Andy the address to an apartment in SoHo on Prince Street. Andy parked a few blocks away from the prewar, six-floor, elevator apartment building. They hustled down the street and under the overhang to the building to get out of the snow and took the elevator to the fourth floor. The dimly lit hallway extended to the last apartment, 4D.

From the other side of the door, music blared. The metal door had a round peephole. Paul knocked and held up his badge. Paul knocked harder. The music abruptly stopped, and the door was yanked open.

Paul stared in surprise at the curly haired, little girl standing in the doorway. He guessed her to be about six. "Is Lacy Knight here?"

The girl frowned. "Lacy's out. What do you want?"

"Is there an adult here with you?" Andy asked, his gaze searching beyond the girl.

"Momma!" the girl yelled, and moved away from the door, leaving it wide open.

Paul shared a look of disbelief and anger with Andy. They could be serial killers. What was this kid doing opening the door to strangers?

A young woman stumbled out from a doorway to the right of the small kitchen. She had the same curly blond hair and blue eyes as the kid. She wore floral flannel pj's and fuzzy slippers. Her eyes widened when she saw Paul and Andy. Paul held up his badge for her to see.

She rushed forward. "Is something wrong? What are

you doing here?" She turned toward the little girl now sitting on the couch tucked under a blanket. "Susie, go into the bedroom."

"Aw, Ma," little Susie huffed but took her blanket and stomped away.

"Ma'am, we're looking for Lacy Knight," Andy stated, his voice harder than normal.

The woman waved her hand. "Lacy's not here. She's staying with her parents uptown. Susie and I are just camping here for a few days."

"And you are?" Paul took out his notepad to record her name.

"Jasmine Oliphant and that's my daughter, Susie."

"How do you know Lacy?" Paul asked.

"We met a few years ago at an AA meeting. Is Lacy in some kind of trouble?"

"No, ma'am. We just have some questions. You said you met at an AA meeting. Is Lacy an alcoholic?"

Jasmine's gaze grew defensive. "Recovering. Just as I am."

Paul made a note of the information in his notepad. "If you could give us her parents' address?" Paul asked, his pen poised to take down the address.

Jasmine's mouth turned down. "I don't know it. I never asked for their address. She works uptown at some art gallery, though."

"Yes, we know." Frustration knocked at Paul's ribs.

He'd have to wait until Lacy came in to work tomorrow to interview her. He flipped his notepad closed. "Sorry to have bothered you."

"No bother." She smiled, two dimples appearing near her mouth.

"Ma'am, I'd suggest you have a stern talk with your daughter about opening doors to strangers," Andy stated. "We wouldn't want to have to come back to find you both raped or murdered."

Jasmine paled. "Yes. Yes, I'll do that."

Paul stared at Andy. He wasn't usually so harsh.

Just as they were stepping into the hall, Paul thought to ask, "Where were you this evening?"

She blinked, her gaze shot up to the right. "Here. Here with Susie."

She was lying.

She was about the right height, blond and blue-eyed, as Rod described. But Rod hadn't mentioned the dimples and they were hard to miss. Looked like Paul would be revisiting Figaro's. "Thank you. Good night."

Back in the sedan, Paul gave his partner a sidelong glance. "What was that about?"

"What?"

"You know what. You deliberately tried to scare that woman." Paul had been just as bugged by the lack of child safety, but Andy's blunt words had taken Paul by surprise.

Andy sighed. "When my sister was about eight, she opened the door. She wasn't as lucky as those two were tonight. Alesha can't have kids now from the attack and she's still plagued with nightmares."

"Oh, man. I didn't know." Empathy for Andy's

pain dug at Paul. Nothing like that had ever touched Paul's life. At least not here in the States. He'd seen more death and destruction during Desert Storm than he'd care to think about.

"Yeah, well. Life goes on and all we can do is try to help others not make the same mistakes," Andy said, his voice grim.

"You got that right," Paul agreed. Fighting in Iraq had been hell on earth. But the war they fought every day in New York City, trying to keep their piece of the world safe, was just as fraught with heartache and devastation as a battlefield.

Sometimes Paul missed the military life. At least then he knew who the enemy was supposed to be. Here…the enemy could be a blue-eyed art curator with a propensity for cleanliness.

"Let's head to the station. I think we've let Ms. McClain cool her heels long enough," Paul stated.

THREE

Megan sat at the square four-by-four metal table, her hands folded on her lap. She tried not to shiver beneath her wool coat, but the room was cold. Cold metal table, cold metal chairs and a cold mirrored wall running the length of the room.

She wondered if the mirror really was two-way, like in the movies. Was someone watching her right now? She couldn't control the spasmodic trembling coursing within her.

Averting her gaze from the mirror, she stared beyond the barred windows to the snow silently falling, the fluffy flakes visible in the streetlight illuminating the back alley of the police station.

When were they going to come in or let her go? She rubbed her hands together, the rough skin chafing. She hadn't worn a watch lately. One of Dr. Miller's therapies. They were trying to break her constant need to know the time to the exact second. Without a watch, the passage of time didn't seem nearly as vexing on most days, but tonight the waiting seemed endless.

Finally, the only door to the room opened and in walked Detective Wallace, his sandy-blond hair damp from the outside weather. His green eyes glittered in the fluorescent light overhead and his firm jaw held his mouth closed in a tight line.

Another man entered the room. The other detective who had been at the gallery. She couldn't remember if she'd heard his name. He was tall and intimidating, yet his dark eyes weren't nearly as hard as his partner's as he stared at her.

"Ms. McClain, let's go over your statement from the crime scene," Detective Wallace said as he sat in a metal chair opposite her across the table. He flipped open the notebook in his hand.

"You were working alone when the two men came in, is that correct?"

Tired and irritable, not to mention freaked out by being locked in an interrogation room for what seemed like hours, she stared at the detective for a moment. "Yes. That is correct. Do I need a lawyer?"

The detective stilled. His green gaze met hers. "If you feel the need for one."

Did she? She didn't know. And she hadn't the foggiest who she'd call. She didn't know any lawyers. But her brother Brody would. She inwardly cringed. The last thing she wanted was to drag her brothers into this. Then they'd start trying to take over and she'd lose the independence she'd fought so hard for these past seven years. No, she could and would control this situation.

Rolling her shoulders to relax the stiff muscles,

she said, "No. No lawyer. I didn't do anything that would require me having a lawyer."

"Good. Then let's go over your statement."

Resigning herself to reiterating the same story again, she nodded and proceeded to answer the detective's questions. Occasionally, the other detective would pipe in with a statement or question. Megan held on to her patience until she thought she'd scream.

"Okay, I think that's good for now," Detective Wallace declared finally as he flipped his notebook closed. "You're on a very short list because your statement has never varied."

"Because I'm telling the truth, Detective."

He eyed her as if she was a life-form he'd never encountered. In this place, maybe he hadn't.

"Can I go home now?" she asked, badly needing to curl up beneath her comforter and forget this whole ordeal, though that wasn't a realistic expectation.

She doubted she'd ever forget this night or be able to banish from her mind the horrible images of those two poor, dead men.

Detective Howell left the room as Detective Wallace stood and came around to help her up. For a second her legs felt wobbly from sitting for so long. When he took hold of her elbow, she reflexively stiffened momentarily.

She didn't like to be touched, but his firm grasp was somehow comforting as he led her out of the interrogation room and into the squad room. Uneasy surprise washed through her. What was different about him?

"Just a second," he said, and released her arm.

He walked over to where the other detective stood talking to a stunning blond woman in a long wool coat. Megan vaguely recognized her but she couldn't recall why. Probably a patron of the gallery. Megan didn't go anywhere else.

Detective Wallace spoke with Detective Howell, took something the man handed him and then sauntered back to her side.

"I'll drive you home," he stated, and gestured for her to precede him to the stairwell.

She was suddenly anxious to escape from his disturbing presence. "Oh, you don't have to do that," she protested as she hurried down the stairs. "I can walk. It's not that far."

As they hit the bottom stair, his hand on the push bar of the double doors leading outside, he gave her an incredulous stare. "I am *not* letting you walk home this late at night and in a storm. If you won't let me drive you, I'll hail you a cab."

She recognized the harsh determined tone of his voice that told her arguing wouldn't do any good. Her brothers all used that same tone when they were set on making her comply with their will. She bristled, desperately wanting to assert her independence and rebuke the detective.

No way was she going to allow him to have control over her life.

But logic prevailed. It *was* late and it *was* freezing outside. She was her own woman. But she wasn't stupid. And she could not do a cab. The very thought sent a shudder through her.

"A ride would be appreciated. Thank you," Megan said as graciously as she could muster.

She thought she detected a smile playing at the corner of his mouth as he pushed open the door and led her to a brown sedan parked near the entrance. He hustled around to the passenger-side front door and opened it for her.

Surprised that she didn't have to sit in the back like a criminal, she slid into the seat and was grateful when he closed the door against the cold elements.

As soon as he pulled the car onto the road, he cranked the heat. She held her hands to the vent in front of her.

"Do I need to give you my address or do you already know it?" she asked, slanting him a glance. His profile showed a sloping forehead, a strong nose and a well-shaped mouth that was particularly handsome as he curved it into a smile.

Though he kept his eyes straight ahead, he answered, "I have the address."

"Figured as much," she muttered. Did he know everything about her? Did he know about Dr. Miller? Apprehension clenched in her gut. Would he use that against her?

Within moments he'd driven the ten blocks to her apartment building. "You're not far from the gallery," he commented as he turned off the engine.

"No. It makes walking to work easier," she replied.

He jumped out and came around to open her door, again showing gentlemanly tendencies, which were very much at odds with the hard image he worked to project. A swoosh of frigid air hit her as she stepped onto the wide sidewalk running the length of the block.

Taking her by the elbow, he walked with her to the door.

She paused at the entrance. "You don't have to come any farther."

He arched a dark blond eyebrow. "Do you have something to hide?" he said with a hint of humor in his voice.

She blinked. Was he teasing? Or just trying to trip her up? "Is this an official visit?"

Fine lines bracketed his mouth. "Not yet."

She swallowed back the panic at the implication she still wasn't in the clear.

His expression grew serious. "I would like to make sure you're safely in your apartment before I leave."

Why did she detect a hint of worry in those green eyes?

Did he think, as she had, that if she hadn't gone looking for her boss she, too, would be dead?

Did he think the killer might come after her?

Whoa! She was letting her imagination run too fast and was tripping on the questions bombarding her mind. The men's deaths had nothing to do with her. She wasn't in danger. God had saved her by sending her in search of her boss. But still…taking precautions was the smart thing to do. She took a deep, calming breath.

"I'd appreciate that," she said, and hurried inside. Safety was safety.

The lobby was decorated in a cheery holiday motif. A tall, fake evergreen with brightly colored ornaments had replaced the cushioned seating near the wall to the right. The doorman, an older fellow of Greek descent, waved from his seat behind a high marble counter. Megan waved back and led the way to the elevator, which was paneled in rich wood.

When the elevator doors opened on the sixth floor, they stepped into the carpeted hall, which was well lit by the many wall sconces. She led him to her apartment and opened the door with her key.

Just as he moved to step inside, she threw out a hand to halt him. "Shoes, please, Detective."

His brows twitched with surprise, then he shrugged as he slipped out of his black dress shoes. With a hand on his holstered gun at his side, he padded in his black socks into her apartment.

She took a tension-filled breath as she waited and mentally whispered her mantra, "When I'm afraid, I'll trust in the Lord."

Detective Wallace came back to the doorway. "All clear."

Relief rushed into her lungs. Of course it was all clear.

Even so, she pushed past him, coming to an abrupt halt at the edge of the throw rug over the hardwood entryway. Her gaze scanned the room. The soft beige couch pushed up against the cream-colored wall, the entertainment center closed, hiding the television she rarely watched and the stereo system her brother Ryan had bought her for a housewarming present, were all as she'd left them.

Her small kitchen sparkled in the soft overhead lights. A dozen fresh roses, all perfect buds, graced the round dining table in a clear Waterford vase.

"I checked the bedroom and the bath," Detective Wallace said.

She hadn't heard him move so close. She nearly jumped out of her skin as she stepped back, putting space between them. "Thank you, Detective."

"Nice place," he stated, his gaze direct, open, nothing like it had been before.

"I like it," she said. Why was he still standing in her apartment? She wasn't used to having guests. "Is there something else you needed?"

A momentary flash of uncertainty entered his green eyes. "No." He gave a short laugh, as if to cover his hesitation. "I should go."

He spun around and put a hand on the doorjamb as he slipped one foot back into his dress shoe.

A choking sensation gripped Megan. She suddenly didn't want to be alone with her memories of the night. She didn't want the detective to leave.

"Detective, would you like to stay for some tea?" she asked quickly before all the reasons why she shouldn't invite him to stay crowded into her consciousness.

He turned to face her, his expression charmingly

earnest. "I'd love some. Anything decaf. And please, call me Paul." He removed his foot from his shoe and shrugged out of his overcoat.

Quickly, she unzipped her boots and placed them on the shelf of the shoe rack beside the door. Then she grabbed the antibacterial, deodorizing, lemon-scented spray from the bottom shelf and gave each boot a quick squirt, as well as the green bootie slippers next to them. When done, she eased her feet into the slippers.

She looked up to find the detective's curious gaze fastened on her face. A flush of embarrassment heated her neck but she refused to give in to the need to explain. She'd been working hard with Dr. Miller to accept that she had some habits that were unusual.

She hurriedly grabbed the detective's coat from where he'd laid it on the Louis VII high-back chair on the other side of the door. "I'll just hang this up."

She hung the damp, brown, London Fog overcoat up in the hall closet and then hung her own wool coat next to it.

After boiling water in her electric kettle, she handed him a basket full of herbal teas to choose from.

He picked cinnamon spice and dipped the bag in his hot water. She chose peppermint for its soothing qualities. And she really needed the calming effect. Her stomach was a riot of nerves. She couldn't believe she was sitting here at her dining table with a man, much less a cop. She'd never had a guest before except her family.

For a tense moment neither spoke. Finally, because she was curious about him, she asked, "Why did you become a detective?"

He stared into his tea. "You know, my family wonders the same thing."

"They must worry about you." She knew firsthand how dangerous the life of a cop could be.

"I'm sure they do." He stretched out his legs, bumping hers in the process.

She stifled the urge to move her leg from his warm one, but soon she let herself relax. If he noticed, he didn't show it.

His index finger skimmed the rim of his mug. "I grew up in Yonkers, very middle class. Mom's a schoolteacher, and Dad's a postal worker. After high school I had no direction, so I enlisted in the marines and after my tour was up, I joined NYPD. Just seemed the way to go."

He was a marine. She hadn't expected that. He certainly hadn't kept his honey-blond hair in a regulation crew cut. She rather liked the way the ends curled, even though his full hair was cut short, just below his ears. She could picture him letting it grow longer. He was a man who'd be able to pull off longer hair without it looking feminine or scruffy. Dragging her thoughts away from his hair, she asked, "Did you serve overseas?"

A shadow entered his eyes. "Yes. Desert Storm."

Her heart clenched. "I still lived at home during that time. My older brother Patrick would sit for hours watching the television broadcast of the bombings. I couldn't watch. It hurt my heart. Being there must have been so hard for you."

He looked away. "It was. But not as hard as it is for our men and women over there now." His gaze swung back to her. "Sometimes…sometimes I think I should go back."

His softly spoken confession touched her deeply and at the same time made her sad that he would want to go back to such a dangerous place. Did he not realize how valuable he was now? "What you do here, in the city, is important. We need good police officers."

"That's what my sister keeps telling me," he said, the tension easing from his gaze.

"How many siblings do you have?" She drank from her mug, the cooling peppermint filling her senses.

"I've a kid sister. She's married and has a five-year-old daughter, Zoe. And you?"

"Three brothers. Two are older and one younger." A thought occurred to her. She narrowed her gaze. "But you probably already know that, right? I assume you did a background check."

He sipped from his tea before answering. "I did. I know that your father was a respected Boston officer and that he died in the line of duty. I know you have three brothers and a mother who still lives in Boston. But reports are dry. I'd rather hear your story from you."

She bit her lip, uncomfortable with the direction in which the conversation was veering. He watched her for a moment and she wondered if she had the word *avoidance* flashing over her head.

Dr. Miller was forever saying she used avoidance too often. That she should step out of her comfort zone, take risks. Talking about her family shouldn't be that hard. She loved them all and was very proud of them.

"I don't know where to start," she said. If she opened up to him, would he then consider her less of a suspect?

"How old were you when your father died?" he asked gently.

Talk about diving in. "I was eight. Too young to really grasp all the nuances of his death. One day he was there and the next not. I knew something bad had happened, though. My brother Brody was with our father when he was murdered." Her heart still ached for Brody. For what he'd witnessed.

"I thought—" Paul frowned. "The report read your father was shot in the line of duty."

She nodded as tears choked her. "Yes. Dad had picked Brody up from school, and they were on their way home when a call came over the radio. They were close." She dropped her gaze to the pine table and traced the grain lines with her finger. "My dad responded."

Paul's hand slid over hers, warm and reassuring. "I'm sorry."

She stared at his bigger hand covering hers, his touch calming, and amazingly she didn't itch to snatch her hand away from the contact. Her breathing shortened.

Her doctor would be so proud that she allowed

contact without first ensuring that she didn't touch any germs. "I became very sick not long after. I…"

Her throat constricted, cutting off the words and her air. She couldn't tell him about her OCD. She couldn't take the risk that he wouldn't use that against her in some way or, at the very least, view her with pity.

Forcing her lungs to open and to receive a breath, she slowly withdrew her hand. When she went to pick up her mug, she found she was shaking. She quickly set the mug down and folded her hands together.

"Megan, are you okay?"

The sincere concern in his voice brought burning tears to the back of her eyes. "I think I'm tired and emotionally spent."

"Of course you are," he said as he scooted his chair away from the table. "Is there someone you can call to come stay with you?"

She shook her head, despairing that she hadn't taken Dr. Miller's advice and made close friends. But she liked her life the way it was.

She had a job she loved, a job that took almost all of her time. She lived in an apartment that was comfortable. She ordered her groceries once a week, did any other shopping online. She lived a very nice, quiet life.

But now something very ugly had intruded.

"I'll be fine, really," she assured him.

"You've had a shock tonight, maybe you should call your family."

"Yes. I will." She rose and moved toward the closet. "I'll get your coat."

She opened the closet door and reached in to take his coat off the hanger. As she pulled the coat forward the hem snagged on something. She tugged.

A brown paper–wrapped package fell forward and landed on her foot.

Shock slammed a tight fist into her gut.

She blinked, praying that the package wasn't what she thought it was. But deep inside she knew it was. The fist squeezed.

"Uh, Detective? Uh…I have a problem here."

Awareness slipped over her in tingling waves as he came to her side. She stared into his inquiring gaze and then pointed to the package that rested at her foot.

She heard his stunned intake of breath. She held hers.

"Is that…?" he asked, his voice whisper soft.

Feeling like her world was madly spinning like a child's toy, she nodded. "I'm afraid so. The Wahlberer."

A heavy hand descended on her shoulder. "I think now you need a lawyer."

FOUR

Paul looked at the brown package resting against Megan's foot and couldn't believe he'd allowed her to suck him in like that. Sucked in by Megan's consistency in telling her story, sucked in by her quirky charm and, yes, even by the fact that he found her incredibly attractive.

But could she really be faking the shock so evident on her pretty face and in her striking blue eyes?

He didn't think so. But was he willing to risk his life on it?

His gaze dropped to the oh-so-incriminating painting propped against her foot. Something was going on, and he was determined to get to the bottom of the situation. But first he had to follow procedure.

"You know I have to arrest you now. Your Miranda rights still apply here, Megan," he stated, though it ripped at his insides to do so.

When she didn't respond, he said, "Listen to me carefully, Megan." He had to get them both out of the apartment because the premises were a crime scene. "Gently lower the painting to the floor and back away."

"Back away?" she repeated, her voice small and reedy.

He took her by the shoulders. "Lower the painting."

Slowly, she withdrew her foot and the painting came to rest on the floor of the closet.

"Good." He applied gentle pressure to her shoulders. "Now back away."

She stepped back. He reached past her for his trench coat. Then he propelled her toward the front door. She reached for the knob. He captured her hand.

"We've contaminated the scene enough," he said, and pulled out a pair of rubber gloves from the inside pocket of his coat. He slipped one on and opened the door.

"But I can't go out in my slippers," she protested, her eyes wide, her pupils dilated.

"I can't let you disturb the scene any more than we've already done," he stated.

When they'd cleared the threshold of the apartment, he used his cell phone to call the station. After explaining the situation to dispatch, he clicked the phone closed. Now they had to wait.

"What are we doing?" Megan asked.

She looked so confused and vulnerable. He resisted the urge to take her in his arms. He had to stay objective. "We wait for the CSI team."

"And then?"

Regret lay heavy across his shoulders. "I have to take you in."

"What? Why? I didn't put that painting in my closet. Why would I do that? Besides I've been in your custody all night." The incredulous expression on her lovely face tore at him.

"Look, Megan, I have a job to do. I have to arrest you for suspicion of murder and theft. If the charges stick or not is up to the courts."

She stared at him with wounded eyes. "Right. The job," she said, and lapsed into stony silence.

Twenty minutes later, the ding of the elevator echoed off the walls. Soon a team of CSI techs descended upon Megan's apartment along with a uniformed officer. Barbara Sims raised an eyebrow at Paul as she walked up.

"Detective, you're keeping us busy tonight," Sims stated, her avid curiosity evident in the way her gaze shifted from Paul to Megan and back.

Paul forced himself not to move protectively closer to Megan. Remember, objectivity, he silently chided himself. "Yes. Busy night. You'll find my prints on the table and on one of the mugs."

One side of the older woman's mouth twitched. "You can take your charge to the station. We've got this."

One glance at Megan's pale face and horrified expression told Paul she didn't like having people going through her apartment. But who would?

The techs were using black dusting powder to lift

prints, combing through the rugs and contents of the closet for any evidence that might help in identifying who may have left the painting.

Assuming that Megan herself hadn't. He hoped she hadn't but then again… He slanted her a glance. Was her shocked innocence an act or real?

Slipping his trench coat over Megan's shoulders, he led her to the elevator. She stepped away from him inside the small space and seemed to withdraw into herself. He regretted she'd ruin her slippers but it couldn't be helped.

When they emerged on the lobby floor, Paul halted. Another uniformed officer stood waiting. The flashing blue strobe lights of a police cruiser bounced off the marbled walls and slashed across the Christmas tree.

Paul led Megan to the officer. To Megan he said, "I need to talk to the doorman."

She nodded. He hesitated, hating to see how inwardly she'd retreated; even her eyes seemed to have dulled. But he had to talk with the doorman, who was staring at them with a great deal of concern showing on his weathered face.

Paul approached, showed his badge and then asked, "Mr.…?"

"Ambrose Theophilus," the doorman replied.

Paul took out his notebook and pen to write down the doorman's name. "Mr. Theophilus, had anyone else come to visit Ms. McClain today?"

The man shook his head. "No. At least not on my

shift." His olive skin blanched slightly as his gaze swung to where Megan and the officer stood waiting. "Is Ms. McClain all right?"

"Who was on shift before you?" Paul asked.

"That would have been Bob Rider. His shift is from noon to six. Mine is from six to midnight."

Making note of this, he asked, "Did you see Ms. McClain tonight before she came in with me?"

"Yes. She rushed in around seven. But she was only in the building for a short time before she rushed back out."

Paul's chest tightened with wary suspicion and disbelief. "Do you have security cameras?"

The doorman nodded. "The lobby is monitored through an off-site security company. I'm sure the building manager would be able to get you the video." His voice dropped a notch. "Did she do something wrong?"

Paul hoped not, but the situation didn't support his gut feeling that what was seen on the surface wasn't really the truth. "I'll need the security company's info as well as the building manager's."

Theophilus picked up a Rolodex and plucked out two cards to hand to Paul. One was for the security company and the other the building manager. Paul tucked the cards into his pocket. "When Ms. McClain came in earlier this evening, did you get a good look at her face?"

Theophilus frowned and thought for a moment. "No, can't say that I did. And she didn't wave as she usually does. But I just figured she was in a hurry, plus her hands were full."

Paul's grip on the pen tightened. "Full?"

"Yeah, she was carrying a big package. I called out, asked if she needed help and she shook her head and disappeared into the elevator."

A big package. Though he'd anticipated the answer, a sharp fist of dread still slammed into Paul's gut. He glanced over to Megan. She had her head down and looked so fragile inside his coat, which hung on her. Could he be wrong? Had she really committed those murders and stolen the painting?

He hated the conflicted thoughts running through his mind. He usually wasn't this unable to judge a situation. With Megan, nothing was adding up on either side of guilt or innocence.

But it wasn't his job to make that determination. He could only deal with the facts. And the fact was Megan appeared guilty. He had probable cause to arrest her.

He thanked the doorman and then hustled Megan back to the sedan. The silent ten-block ride to the station stretched Paul's nerves taut. He parked near the redbrick building's entrance and then came around the passenger side to open Megan's door.

As she emerged, he could see her lips moving, though she made no sound. He touched her elbow; she flinched away, which for some reason bugged him.

Thankfully the snow had abated as they started toward the side stairs. He realized that Megan was walking strangely, putting the heel of one foot to the toe of the other, stepping, then repeating the process, the way someone does when they're measuring a space. She took the stairs and then continued her measuring walk to the blue double doors of the Nineteenth Precinct station house.

He held the door for her to pass through. The warmth enveloped them as they stepped inside. Megan slipped the too-large coat off and held it out to him. Paul took the coat; the fresh scent of her shampoo clung to the fabric.

Desk Sergeant Rita Rosario leaned on the high counter she worked behind. "Hey, Wallace, heard you were bringing back the art lady."

"Is there a room open?" he asked, ignoring her comment.

"Three." Rita gestured with her head.

"Thanks," Paul said as he led Megan toward an interrogation room. He opened the door and escorted her inside. Megan moved to the far corner of the small room. Her arms were wrapped around her middle and she shivered like a leaf in a strong breeze.

"Are you sure you don't want to keep my coat on you?"

Her gaze pierced him. "No."

He sighed. "Fine. Have a seat. I'll be right back."

Instead of heading to the chief's office, or even calling his partner, Andy, Paul went straight to his locker where he kept an extra set of clothes for times when he couldn't make it back to his West Side apartment. He had dress clothes as well as his gym stuff. He grabbed a clean pair of athletic socks and a sweatshirt with Yonkers High School emblazoned across the front.

On his way back to the interrogation room, he stopped at his desk and called Andy to let him know what was going on. Then he checked to see if Chief Erickson had returned from informing the families of the victims. The chief's office was dark.

Paul entered the interrogation room with his offering. Megan had sat in the chair, but still appeared cold despite the heat pouring in through the vents. He set the sweatshirt and socks on the table beside her. She gave him a questioning stare.

"They're clean," he stated.

She turned her gaze to the clothes and for a long moment didn't move. Then slowly, she reached out to take the socks. She shook them out as if to make sure no insects inhabited them. She kicked off her slippers and proceeded to put her feet into the socks. Then she grabbed the gray sweatshirt and put it on. "Thank you," she said.

"You're entitled to a phone call," Paul said, his voice bouncing off the stuccoed walls.

"I'd like to make one," she said, her voice steady, determined.

He led her to an unoccupied desk to use the phone. He moved a discreet distance away to give her privacy.

When she was done with her call, she turned to him. "My brother is posting whatever bail is necessary and hiring a lawyer."

Glad that her family was taking care of her, Paul wasn't sure what to do with her. He couldn't bring himself to take her to a holding cell. Instead, he took her back to the interrogation room. She silently resumed her seat.

"Would you like something to eat or drink?" he asked.

"I'd just like to be left alone until my brother comes," she replied in a chilly voice, her gaze downcast and her hands folded in her lap.

Disconcerted by how badly he wished he could make this situation better for her, Paul withdrew from the room, but he felt like he was abandoning her.

And that wasn't a good feeling at all.

Megan hated sitting in that awful, cramped room waiting. She still couldn't believe someone had stashed the Wahlberer painting in her apartment. Who would do such a thing? The same person who killed those two men, that's who. But why put the painting in her closet? For that matter, why use her packing scissors to kill one of the men? None of the events of the night made any sense to her.

Not the murders, the painting or Detective Wallace.

She wasn't sure where he stood. Did he believe her guilty or innocent? When she'd first met him, there was no doubt in her mind that he'd thought her capable of such evil. But then he seemed to have shifted his attitude, and she'd really felt like they were connecting in a way she had never connected with anyone other than her family. After she'd found the painting, his green eyes had glowed with doubts. Her heart twisted with despair.

She really wanted him to believe in her. Though why she wasn't sure. Maybe it was her pragmatic side or perhaps, because she'd enjoyed the time with him and hated to think of him believing the worst of her.

She breathed deep, trying to alleviate the pounding at her temples. Soon her brother would be here and then she'd have even more problems to deal with. Like how to convince her siblings that as soon as they helped her out of this mess she shouldn't be shipped back home to be put under the watchful eye of their mother. Megan had worked too hard for her independence to lose it now.

Ever since she'd been struck with her illness, her mother had cocooned her in a protective shield that had made Megan yearn for her own life. As soon as Megan could, she had forged a life for herself despite her difficulties.

And now that was threatened.

Well, she wouldn't let any of that keep her from living the life she'd cut out for herself. Regardless that there were times she yearned for something more. But she wasn't exactly sure what that more was despite Dr. Miller's assertion what she lacked was companionship.

Okay, maybe she did. For once she did wish she had someone to lean on. But that was what family was for.

Hence, why she'd called her brother Brody.

An hour later, the door to the room opened and a woman wearing a tailored dress suit walked in. Megan stared in surprise as the woman put her brown leather briefcase on the table and stuck out her hand.

"I'm Hillary Gibberman, your lawyer," the woman stated in a very authoritative tone. Her short, stylish, blond hair showed signs of graying at the temples, and her sharp midnight-blue eyes were direct.

Megan forced herself to shake the hand offered to her even as a shudder coursed through her because she didn't have any antibacterial wipes and no way of knowing if Ms. Gibberman's hand was clean. Dr. Miller would be so proud of her. "Did my brother send you?"

"Yes, your brother Patrick called me. I then spoke with your brother Brody who filled me in. I've just spoken with both Detective Wallace and Chief Erickson. Your bail has been paid, so let's get you out of here. Your brothers will be arriving tomorrow. But for tonight I'll get you set up in a hotel."

Megan took in a painfully sharp breath. "A hotel? I can't do that. Why can't I go back to my apartment?"

Hillary raised her eyebrows. "Well, you certainly could go back there. The CSI team has released the scene. I just assumed you'd be more comfortable in a hotel since someone obviously broke into your apartment to plant the painting."

Though she hated the idea of someone having intentionally placed the packaged Wahlberer in her apartment, Megan knew she couldn't stay anywhere else. "I'll be fine as long as I can go to my apartment."

She cracked a smile. "That's what your brother said you'd say. All right, then. Shall we?" Hillary motioned toward the door.

Megan rose and moved to follow her lawyer. "Uh, I don't have any shoes."

Hillary paused as she opened the door. "My word, you sure don't." She marched forward and straight to Detective Wallace. "My client needs her shoes to return to her apartment."

Megan caught Paul's gaze. There was apology in his green eyes, which made her pulse jump slightly. He held up her soggy slippers. "She came in these." He sidestepped around Hillary to speak to Megan. "I have a pair of running shoes you can borrow to get home in."

She swallowed back the trepidation of wearing someone else's shoes. Even Paul's. But she couldn't very well walk out in the socks on her feet. Her only other option was the wet slippers. Soggy won out. She latched on to the slippers. "I'll just make do with these."

He nodded, his expression tight, and let go. She quickly tucked her feet into the cold slippers.

"I'll escort you back to your apartment," Paul stated.

"That won't be necessary, Detective," Hillary stated as she crowded in, hovering over Megan in a protective way. "My driver will take Ms. McClain home."

As Megan followed Hillary to the stairs, she couldn't help but glance back at Paul. He gave her a salute before turning away. Megan tried to understand the disappointment and yearning that gripped her.

She should be glad to be going home, but she felt very alone without Paul by her side. Hmm. That was weird.

Pushing away the unwanted sensation, she hurried after Hillary to the black Lincoln Town Car waiting at the curb. Megan slid onto the backseat. She scooted to the far side when Hillary joined her.

"So did you do it?" Hillary's eyes pinned Megan to the seat.

Aghast that she would even ask, Megan answered with a vehement, "No."

Hillary's assessing gaze sharpened for a moment then softened. "Good. I'll get the arraignment scheduled and start working on your defense in the morning. You'll come to my office at ten tomorrow."

Megan swallowed. "My defense?"

Hillary waved a hand. "Don't worry, I've yet to let an innocent defendant go to jail."

Somehow Hillary's confidence didn't reassure Megan. And as soon as the Town Car came to a halt in front of her building she had the door open and was climbing out.

Hillary said, "Remember. 10:00 a.m."

Megan nodded and closed the car door. The cold of the snowy sidewalk seeped through her slippers as she hustled inside. Mr. Theophilus had already gone for the evening, and since Megan never went out late at night she didn't recognize the younger doorman sitting behind the desk. "Can I help you?"

"McClain, apartment 6C," she said, staring at his pierced nose.

He waved her in and she rushed to the elevator. Once inside her apartment, she took a moment to assess the damage done by the crime-scene investigators. Black soot marred most of the surfaces, her items were in a haphazard disarray. She shuddered at the chaos around her. She fought the urge to clean up as exhaustion overtook her.

Holding her hands to the sides of her eyes to block her view, she made a beeline for her bedroom. Here there were signs of her things being moved around as the investigators looked for evidence or whatever they looked for.

But the extent of the invasion in her room wasn't nearly as bad as the rest of her apartment; the only area mucked with black powder was the window and sill. She straightened the pillow on the reading chair by the window, adjusted the Persian throw rug back to its original position and smoothed out the covers of her bed.

As she removed Paul's sweatshirt, she was engulfed in the fresh, clean scent of his laundry soap that clung to the fabric.

She breathed in, savoring the way his scent reminded her of how she'd felt warm and cared for when he offered up his socks and sweatshirt. Neatly, she folded the shirt and placed the garment on the top of a stack of folded laundry waiting to be washed.

After changing into her nightclothes and completing her nightly Bible study, Megan cocooned herself beneath her covers and prayed she'd be able to sleep.

Both men each carried in a large duffel-style bag. Megan raised an eyebrow. It looked like they'd packed enough for a week, not just an overnight stay as she'd have expected. Trepidation crept up her spine. "Where are you two staying? And for how long?"

The two brothers exchanged a glance.

Brody set his bag on the floor at his feet and widened his stance.

Uh-oh, Megan thought. When Brody got that look on his face that said "this is how it is" she knew she wasn't going to like their answer.

Patrick carried his bag to the couch. Then slowly he came back to take Megan's hand. "We think it would be best if you go home to Boston when this is all over."

Anger spurted through her veins. She yanked her hand away. "No. This is my home."

"Boston has art galleries. Besides, Mom could use the company now that I'm living in Florida and Ryan's living in Hawaii. Brody and Kate have their hands full with Joseph," Patrick stated.

She'd just known they'd do this. That they'd try talk her into giving up the independence, the life 'd worked so hard for. And playing the guilt card their mother was alone wouldn't work. Their er was a strong and independent person who bly was enjoying that her kids were finally heir own lives.

les, Megan was doing well. Better than she ars. Okay, maybe as of last night not so sidering she was a suspect in a double

As she drifted off, it wasn't the gruesome murder scene that occupied her mind, but the handsome face of the homicide detective and his suspicious, disappointed green eyes.

Megan awoke to a pounding in her head. She curled tighter into a ball beneath her covers, willing the throbbing noise to go away. It didn't.

The veracity of the incessant noise increased.

Someone was at her front door.

Throwing off the covers, she grabbed her thick terry-cloth robe and put on her matching pink slippers before padding through the cold air of her apartment. As she passed the thermostat, she flicked the on button. By the time she reached the door the vents were buzzing with the sound of heated air.

One glance through the peephole and Megan knew her day was going to be a whopper and it wasn't even 8:00 a.m.

Plucking an antibacterial wipe from the canister sitting on the shoe rack, she wrapped the moist towelette around the doorknob and opened the door.

On the threshold stood two of her brothers. She'd expected Brody, but not her eldest brother, Patrick. Her younger brother, Ryan, was still in Hawaii on the island of Maui. But he was bringing his fiancée home for Patrick's New Year's Day "second" wedding, since Patrick and his wife, Anne, had had to sneak off to Vegas for their nuptials while Anne was still in the federal witness protection program.

Anne had witnessed the murder of her employer by a known crime syndicate boss. She'd entered the witness protection program and moved to Boston where, while in disguise, she worked at the college where Patrick was a professor.

Now that the threat to Anne's life was gone, Patrick and Anne were free not only to live their lives, but to have a "real" wedding.

Tears welled in Megan's eyes and clogged her throat. She launched herself into her eldest brother's arms even though the scowl on his handsome face and the worry so evident in his brown eyes behind his wire-rimmed glasses were all about her and the situation she'd found herself in. It was just so good to see her big brother.

Patrick hugged her back. "Hey, now. Don't start crying on me, you'll ruin my suit."

She laughed. "I don't think even my tears could damage this solid tweed," she remarked as she pulled back to look at him. Taller than the rest of the siblings, Patrick looked the most like their father. A pang of sadness hit her like it always did when she thought of her father and all that she and her family had missed out on because of the man who murdered him.

"Hey, Anne likes my tweed," Patrick replied dryly.

Megan was glad to know her big brother had finally found the right person for him. Their mother had despaired that Patrick would never have a life of his own.

Brody edged closer. "Don't I get a hug?"

"Of course," Megan answered and transferred her affection to her next eldest brother. She was surprised not to see him in his brown sheriff's uniform; instead he looked ruggedly handsome in his jeans and thick plaid shirt. He was rock solid and steady now that he'd forged a life for himself and his family in Havensport on the Nantucket Sound.

Brody had been the one most affected by their father's murder, having witnessed it. He'd gone into law enforcement as a way to find some justice and peace with the tragedy. But then he'd been shot by the woman who professed to love him, and his heart had hardened not only to love but to God.

Megan still marveled that Brody had found love again with a strong, courageous and godly woma[n] like Kate, who'd had her own issues to deal wi[th] when they met; she'd been a suspect in her [ex-]husband's murder. Brody and Kate had worke[d to]gether to solve her ex-husband's murder, disc[overed] her ex-husband had been connected to the [ ] mafia. Together they managed to take do[wn the bad] guys and fell in love in the proces[s. They] married in a beachside ceremony a f[ ] and had a precious little boy name[d]

Megan held on to Brody's [ ] rested her cheek against his h[ ] thud of his heart soothed he[r]

"Are you going to inv[ite]" asked.

Reluctantly, Mega[n] back. "Of course. Com[e]

homicide and a theft, but aside from that, her life was working.

"No. I'm sure Mom is just fine. I like it here. I'm not leaving."

Patrick sighed and looked at Brody. "I told you she wouldn't leave."

Brody's dark eyes regarded her with determination. "Yes, you did. So, Meggie, we're staying here until this mess is resolved."

"Here?" she squeaked. "As in my apartment?"

Both brothers nodded.

A boulder-size hunk of doom settled on Megan's chest. "I don't think so."

"We have an appointment with Hillary Gibberman at ten. I suggest you go get ready while we make some breakfast. I'm starved. They didn't have much worth eating on the train in," Brody stated.

Patrick nodded. "Same here. The flight from Orlando had a granola bar and a banana."

Megan stared aghast at her brothers. She loved them to pieces, but at the moment she wanted to scream. She'd worked too hard and too long to lose control of her life.

She retreated to her room to cool off. She'd have to figure out a plan to get them to leave sooner rather than later. Maybe after the meeting with the lawyer her brothers would feel reassured that she would be fine without their interference in her life.

A half hour later, when she emerged dressed in navy slacks and a red turtleneck with her long dark hair held back in a clip, she found Brody dishing up their plates. The wonderful smells of bacon, eggs and toast made her stomach grumble in response. She took the plate offered her and sat down next to Patrick at the small dinette table.

Brody joined them with his own plate. "So tell us about Detective Wallace."

Megan choked on the piece of bacon she'd just put in her mouth. "Tell you what?"

Brody exchanged a glance with Patrick.

Patrick picked up his mug of coffee and eyed her over the rim, his gaze rife with curiosity. "We heard that you invited him in for tea."

Uh-oh. Now she was in for it.

FIVE

"And then he arrested you," Brody added, his expression thunderous.

Heat crept up Megan's neck. She was not going there with her brothers. Mainly because she didn't know what to say. So she found Paul attractive and engaging when he wasn't looking at her as a suspect.

But she certainly wasn't going to discuss her romantic life, or lack thereof, with her brothers. Besides, Brody shouldn't cast a stone since he'd arrested Kate the first time he met her, and they ended up happily married.

"You know, I better hurry if I'm going to make that appointment with Ms. Gibberman," she said, and stuffed her mouth with food.

"Did Detective Wallace invite himself in?" Brody questioned.

She shook her head and swallowed.

"Because he had no right to search your apartment without a warrant," Brody continued. "The painting as evidence will have to be dismissed."

A lump of dread lodged itself in her chest. She had to tell them she'd invited him in. "He didn't search anything. I invited him in and I found the painting."

"You should have called me before letting the detective know it was in your apartment," Brody admonished.

Megan arched her eyebrow. "How would hiding the painting have helped me?"

When her brother didn't answer but only stared back at her in stony silence, Megan moved to clear the table. "I have to run over to the gallery and ask Lacy to cover for me while I go to this meeting."

Both brothers immediately rose. "We'll go with you," Patrick stated.

Megan waved him off. "You don't have to. It's just across the street."

Brody folded his arms across his chest. "We're going."

Like it not, the two were going to be her oversize shadow for the day. She acknowledged that having them at hand while navigating the judicial system would be less confusing; she could only hope by nightfall they would both realize she was capable enough to continue to live her life and they could leave.

Paul and Andy arrived at the gallery and waited under the blue awning, looking for some shelter from the wind that had kicked up and nipped at Paul's exposed ears. The fast-moving traffic across the lanes of Lexington had long since melted the dusting of powdery snow from the night before and the sky was a dismal shade of gray.

A black Town Car pulled to the curb, and Mr. Sinclair opened the back passenger door and climbed out, pulling his tan cashmere coat tighter around his thin body. A very attractive blonde followed Sinclair out of the car. She wore a long, black duster over a bright red, fashionable pantsuit. She was tall, in her early twenties, with big, round blue eyes.

Paul stepped forward, blocking Sinclair's way.

The older man's gaze narrowed a fraction as if he were assessing a threat, before recognition entered his eyes. "Detective Wallace, has something more happened? I read in this morning's paper that you arrested my art curator."

Paul refrained from commenting on Megan. "We would like to speak to Ms. Knight."

Sinclair gestured to the young blond woman at his side. "Well, as luck would have it, Lacy stopped by the house this morning for coffee and scones."

The blonde stuck out her hand. "Lacy Knight. My uncle told me about what happened last night. It's just so unbelievable."

Paul introduced himself and Andy, then launched into his first question as he took out his notepad. "Where were you last evening?"

Lacy raised her dark blond eyebrows. "Me? I was at home."

"Home being where?" Paul studied her face, looking for telltale signs of deception.

"Home being my parents' house. They live just off the park at Eightieth. I've been staying there because a friend needed a place to crash for a while."

"Gentlemen, can we do this inside?" Sinclair asked as he blew on his uncovered hands.

Flexing his own gloved fingers, Paul asked, "Do you not wear gloves, Mr. Sinclair?"

"I normally do, but I couldn't find them yesterday when I left," Sinclair answered while unlocking the gallery's front door. Paul and Andy followed Sinclair and his great-niece inside. Sinclair disarmed the security system and then led the way upstairs to his office, which in the bright of daylight was more posh than Paul had remembered. Glass and polished-brass fixtures, rich leather chair and floor-to-ceiling windows.

Paul continued with his questions. "Were your parents home with you, Ms. Knight?"

She hitched a hip on the side of Sinclair's glass desk. "No, they were at a charity function."

Paul consulted his notes. "Ms. McClain stated you left before five in the evening for an appointment? What appointment?"

She held out her red-tipped nails. "A mani. Diane at Kim's Nails does the best job in the city."

"Where is Kim's Nails?" Andy asked. "How long did that take?"

She gave a delicate shrug. "An hour. Kim's is on West Fifty-seventh. Then I scooted over to Dean & Deluca to pick up some salads from the deli counter.

From there I went home." A crease appeared between her eyebrows. "Why are you asking me this? You arrested Megan. Do you think she didn't do it? I, for one, just can't see Megan killing anyone, considering how obsessively clean she is."

No kidding. He'd noticed the way she sanitized her shoes and most everything else she touched. "We're gathering all the facts we can," Paul replied. "What was Ms. McClain's relationship to Thomas Drake and Henry Vanderpool?"

A look of bewilderment crossed Lacy's features. "Relationship? I didn't know there was one. Are you saying she was having an affair with one of these men?" Lacy turned to her uncle. "Did you know that?"

Sinclair gave a negative shake of his head.

"I'm not suggesting she was. I was asking if *you* knew of any existing relationship," Paul said as neutrally as possible.

"Oh, no. Not that I would. Megan keeps to herself," Lacy replied as she picked at the cuff of her pantsuit jacket.

Paul shifted his attention to Sinclair. "Who was the blonde at the bar last night?"

Sinclair visibly blanched. "I…" His gaze darted to his niece and then back to Paul. "Just a woman who wanted to talk art. It was nothing worth noting."

"Everything is worth noting in a homicide investigation," Andy stated. "Did you know the woman?"

"No. She stopped me. Said she'd been to the gallery and wanted to find out more about how the gallery worked, how I chose which artists to exhibit. Would I be willing to look at some of her work?"

"Do you have her name?" Andy asked.

Sinclair shook his head. "No. I gave her my card and said she could send me some samples. You don't think she had anything to do with the murders or the theft, do you?"

Paul shrugged noncommittally. "We don't know." He turned his gaze back to Lacy. "What time did you arrive at your parents'?"

"After seven, maybe seven-thirty."

"Can anyone verify your presence in your parents' house at that time?" Andy asked, his dark gaze intense.

Lacy blinked. "No. My parents were already gone by the time I arrived."

Paul made a note to check the neighbors for verification of Lacy's alibi.

From somewhere in the building a door slammed.

"That would be Joanie, the receptionist. She always announces her presence with a bang," Lacy stated dryly.

"We'll need to talk with her as well," Paul said, wondering if Joanie might know more about the personal life of the gallery's curator since her assistant didn't know her very well, which seemed odd.

But so far, everything about this case seemed odd.

According to what the Vanderpool widow told Chief Erickson, her husband was supposed to have been out of town on a business trip. And the Drake widow had said her husband should have been at a dinner business meeting. Neither woman had known about their husband's desire to procure the Wahl-berer painting.

The only true suspect in the murders was the art curator and as of yet, Paul couldn't find a connection between Megan and either of the men. And finding the painting in her apartment seemed too convenient.

After putting together the time line, he just didn't see how she could have killed the two men, rid all the traces of the murders from her person and had time to stash the painting in her closet.

Which was another sticking point for Paul. If she'd put the stolen artwork in her hall closet, why would she have invited him in for tea and, especially, why would she have even opened the closet door?

It didn't make sense. Megan was too smart to trip up like that. Paul's instinct told him someone was setting her up. But who?

Mr. Sinclair? Lacy Knight?

Neither one had a rock-solid alibi.

One of the other employees?

Until he'd questioned them all, he would reserve judgment, because he was confident he'd eventually uncover the truth. He only hoped the truth would reveal that Megan was innocent, because deep inside he was convinced she was.

Megan pulled her coat tighter around her as she walked to the corner of the block, flanked on either side by a brother. Stepping around the piles of dirty snow pushed to the curb, they crossed Lexington and headed down the block to the gallery. A woman wearing a long fur coat pulled open the door and stepped inside the dress shop next to the gallery and snatches of Christmas music floated out.

Festive decorations adorned the shop windows all the way down the street and greenery hung from the streetlamps. Megan hadn't even started her Christmas shopping; she'd been waiting for the upcoming weekend to devote time to sitting in front of her computer and ordering gifts. Her brothers definitely had to leave before then, because sadly she'd come to realize how isolated she'd become and she'd never hear the end of it if they knew.

Brody held open the gallery door for Megan and Patrick to enter. As she stepped inside, Megan's mind flashed with the gruesome scene from the night before. She shuddered and pushed the images away.

Joanie was behind the reception desk. Her pretty brown eyes widened when she saw Megan. In her thirties, married with a middle-schooler, Joanie had been working for the gallery for almost a year. Megan found Joanie's conservative demeanor soothing.

Joanie rushed out from behind the counter but stopped a few paces from Megan and gave her two brothers a curious glance. "Honey, are you all right? I couldn't believe it when I heard about those poor men and then your arrest. It's unfathomable."

"I'm fine," Megan assured her, and introduced her brothers before asking for Lacy.

Joanie waved a hand toward the offices upstairs. "She's with Mr. Sinclair and those detectives."

Megan stilled. "Detectives?" Paul was here?

Brody took her by the arm. "Let's see what's going on."

Megan tried to come up with a plausible excuse for not intruding, but she had to admit she wanted to see Paul again. She led the way to her boss's office on the second floor. The door to the office was open. Paul and his partner had their backs to the door. Megan could see that Paul had his notebook out.

Mr. Sinclair sat at his desk while Lacy faced the officers with a hip hitched on the edge of the desk. Her blond curls had been slicked back today. Her dark red lipstick made the paleness of her skin that much more apparent. Her big, blue, guileless eyes stared at the detectives as she answered their questions.

Patrick knocked on the doorjamb as they stepped inside.

Paul swiveled around, his gaze slamming directly into Megan. She tried not to let the jolt of gladness at seeing him show on her face. The last thing she wanted was for anyone, especially her brothers, to notice the effect Paul had on her.

Brody marched forward. "Detectives, I'm Brody McClain, Megan's brother. And this is Patrick, one of our other brothers."

Paul shook Brody's hand. "Paul Wallace. This is my partner, Andy Howell."

The men all shook hands. Megan marveled at the

ritualistic custom that made her skin itch. She wanted to shoo them all off to the restroom to wash their hands, but she refrained, because it would be so embarrassing. Her brothers were used to her behavior, but not the detectives. She stuck her hands into the pockets of her coat.

Mr. Sinclair stood and came around his desk. "Megan, I was so worried about you."

Megan appreciated his concern. "Thank you. I won't be able to work today and was hoping Lacy could cover for me."

Lacy slid off the desk, her face eager. "Of course I can. We'll be fine without her, won't we, Uncle?"

Mr. Sinclair's gray brows twitched slightly. Megan wondered if in annoyance or amusement.

"Yes, Lacy. For a day or so, we'll manage." He shifted his gaze back to Megan. "I don't believe for a minute that you could have killed those men or stolen the painting. Your job is secure."

"Thank you," she said, hating that she was even suspected of such evilness but grateful for her boss's support. Turning to Lacy, Megan said, "There are just a few things I need to go over with you. We're expecting a sample package from a new artist who'd like to be included in the spring show."

Lacy tucked her hand through Megan's arm and patted her through the heavy wool of Megan's coat. "Don't you worry, Meg. I'll take care of everything."

Megan should have been used to Lacy's demonstrative ways after working with the young woman for the past three years, but Megan still pulled away, requiring Lacy to disengage from her arm. "Thank you, Lacy, I knew I could count on you."

Lacy beamed a smile at her before addressing the police officers. "Detectives, if you are through with your questions, may I get to work?" she asked.

Paul nodded. "You've been most cooperative, Ms. Knight. Thank you. If we have anything further, we'll be in touch."

Megan started for the door.

"Ms. McClain," Paul called out to her.

Megan paused and turned around. "Detective?"

In two long strides he was at her side, crowding her senses; his eyes darkened with worry. She recognized his aftershave, the scent at once soothing, and yet creating a maelstrom of chaotic emotions jumbled in her chest.

She wanted back the tentative camaraderie they'd begun before she'd found the painting; she wanted to see where the relationship could go. Her head told her this man was dangerous to her well-being, but her heart said otherwise.

But the reality was she was a murder suspect and he was a cop. Just like oil and water, their lives could never mix.

"Are you okay?" he asked, his voice low so that only she could hear.

"Yes," she murmured. His concern was heart-swelling and so unexpected.

His gaze searched her face as intimately as a

caress. A little shiver of delight coursed through her. She reached out to touch his arm.

Suddenly Patrick and Brody were there, hovering, closing Paul out in a protective gesture that both annoyed and touched her.

"Megan has given you her statement. From now on she doesn't talk to you without her lawyer," Brody stated, his voice hard-edged as only someone in law enforcement could perfect.

The corners of Paul's mouth lifted slightly as he stepped back. "Of course. I understand."

"Patrick," Megan complained as her older brother took hold of her arm and propelled her toward the door where Lacy stood waiting, lively curiosity dancing in her blue gaze.

"Ladies," Patrick said with a sweeping gesture for them to precede him out the door while Brody brought up the rear.

Lacy staged a whisper to Megan. "Do you and the cop have a thing going on?"

Megan groaned inwardly. "No, of course not," she said, hoping her denial would ward off any more comments from her assistant.

But as they descended the stairs, she chanced a glance at her eldest brother, hoping he hadn't heard Lacy's question. The arched winged eyebrows visible above his glasses spoke volumes.

Great. Now her brothers would be relentless in ferreting out her feelings for Detective Wallace. How could she explain how she felt when she didn't even know herself?

* * *

"What exactly are your intentions toward my sister?"

The question caught Paul off guard. He frowned. Who asked something like that in this day and age?

Paul faced Brody McClain, unsure how to respond when he couldn't say for sure why he'd felt the need to reassure himself that she was okay. Maybe it was the way her big blues stared at him when she'd first arrived, as if she were glad to see him.

So much better than when they'd parted the night before with her lawyer towing her away and her eyes so hurt, as if he'd kicked her puppy or something. That had torn him up inside all night. But he'd had to arrest her. It was his job.

Now staring into the furious gaze of her brother, Paul knew he couldn't let on that he cared. He doubted McClain would believe him. "The only intention I have is finding the truth."

"The truth is my sister could not have done this," McClain insisted.

Though Paul knew he should keep his own opinion close to the vest, he felt compelled to confide in McClain, as one law-enforcement officer to another. Shifting so his back was toward Sinclair and lowering his voice, Paul said, "I tend to agree. My gut tells me someone is setting her up."

Surprise flickered in McClain's gaze. "Okay." McClain glanced over his shoulder toward where Andy was talking to Sinclair. "You think him?"

"Not sure yet," Paul said, unwilling to commit to any suspicions.

"Patrick and I will be staying for a few days but after that she'll need protection."

McClain eyed him with interest and, if Paul wasn't mistaken, approval.

"You'll watch out for her?" McClain asked.

"As best as I can," Paul answered, feeling the weight of commitment on his shoulders. He couldn't promise anything more than that and from the agreement in McClain's eyes, Paul knew the fellow officer of the law understood.

Because as much as Paul hated to admit it, he had a hinky feeling that if Vanderpool hadn't shown up, Megan would have been the second victim.

SIX

"So what was that sidebar chat with the brother about?"

Paul snapped his seat belt in place then looked at Andy. "He's concerned. Wanted to be assured she'll be protected."

Andy arched an eyebrow as he maneuvered the sedan into the morning traffic. Around them, yellow taxis vied for position in the lanes against limousines, Town Cars and other civilian vehicles. Pedestrians waited at the corners, ready to bolt the second the lights turned.

Andy slanted him a glance. "You don't think she did it, do you?"

His gut said no, regardless that his head cautioned against too much confidence. He shook his head. "No. I really don't." He shrugged. "But, hey, I could also be wrong."

Andy shook his head. "You have good instincts."

"But she could be a good actress," Paul countered.

"True. Time will tell," Andy stated.

Paul nodded. "Time will tell. I want to check out the alibi of the receptionist, talk to the day security guards and then check with anyone in the vicinity of Lacy Knight's parents' for verification that she was truly there."

"And I think I'd like to take a photo of Lacy and Jasmine Oliphant to Figaro's, see if either of them was the woman whom Sinclair met at the bar."

"Good idea."

Andy parked in the slot allocated to Homicide. Paul jumped out and hustled inside. They had a full day ahead of them.

"Hey, Paul," Detective Maria Gonzales called out from where she sat at her desk. Her dark, straight hair was pulled back into her traditional ponytail and her olive skin glowed without a stitch of make-up. A few years older than Paul with two school-aged kids, Maria brought a certain elegance to the station house. She exhibited a cool head and calm emotions.

She also had a tough attitude, but cooked the best chocolate cake ever. Paul was sure that if Maria ever left the force, it would be to open her own bakery.

Paul bypassed his own desk to approach Maria. She kicked out the chair beside her and motioned for him to take a seat. Shrugging out of his coat, he turned the chair backward, straddled the seat and draped his coat over the back. "So what's up?"

"How's your investigation going in the art gallery murders?"

"I have some theories. A few parties of interest with shaky alibis," he replied.

"What about Megan McClain? You arrested her, but you're not sure she committed the crime?" Maria's black-as-onyx eyes drilled through Paul.

"I have my doubts," he said, wondering where she was going with this.

She nodded and leaned closer. She lowered her voice to almost a whisper. "Something's up with the widows."

Paul raised his eyebrows. "The chief hadn't mentioned that." Come to think of it, Chief Erickson had been pretty mum earlier in the morning when Paul had asked how it had gone with the widows. The chief had pulled a sad face and spoken of how broken up the two women were. The chief had congratulated Paul on the arrest and assumed the case was closed.

A feeling that Paul couldn't explain had stopped him from voicing his reservations about Megan's guilt.

A feeling that his sister would say was God speaking to him.

He wasn't sure if that was true, but he'd learned to heed that still, small voice inside that gave him direction. Doing so had saved his hide on many occasions.

But why now? With the chief?

He stood, not wanting to continue with the conversation in the house. "Let's go grab some coffee."

Maria rose, grabbing her down jacket and hat before following Paul out of the station and down to the corner diner where they slid into a far, back booth away from any ears that might be interested.

Maria smiled at the waitress as she came to take their orders. "Coffee and a sticky bun."

"Just coffee," Paul said and waited until the waitress was out of earshot. "So spill."

Maria drummed her fingers on the Formica tabletop. "I can't put my finger on exactly what's bothering me about those two widows. The Drake woman was very emotional, but I swear her eyes were cold and she had some bruises on her wrist that she tried to hide with her sleeve. I mentioned them to the chief but he didn't want to go there. He said that Mrs. Drake is the daughter of George Grieger, a multimillionare who backs the mayor, and the less scandal the better."

"Right. Wouldn't want anyone to know his daughter was being abused," Paul stated, his tone dripping with sarcasm. Nothing worse in Paul's book than a man who abused his wife or children. "So you think there's a chance Mrs. Drake was somehow involved in her husband's murder?"

Maria made a face. "I'm not saying that. I just think she wasn't as upset as she tried to make us believe."

Paul fished out his notepad and made a note to follow up with the widow Drake. "What about Vanderpool's widow?"

"Definitely a bit odd," Maria said. "She—"

The waitress approached with their order. After she left, Maria continued, "She cried as one would expect after hearing the news that your husband had been murdered. But what struck me was that when her teenage daughter started downstairs, Mrs. Vanderpool was quick to shoo her back up. Then Mrs. Vanderpool hustled us out faster than a Yankee spitball."

"Maybe she didn't want to tell the daughter with an audience," Paul suggested as he sipped from his coffee.

Maria put creamer in her mug and stirred. "Maybe. Shelia offered to stay and help break the news, but Mrs. Vanderpool was adamant she didn't need help."

"Some people don't feel comfortable with a psychologist," Paul commented. "Did Mrs. Vanderpool know why her husband had gone to the gallery?"

Maria shook her head. "No. He was supposed to be at a business dinner. She didn't know anything about the painting."

"And Mrs. Drake?" Paul asked.

"She did know about the painting. She'd asked him to buy it for her mother's upcoming birthday."

"So why had Mr. Vanderpool gone to the gallery?" Paul said, his mind going over what Megan had stated: that Vanderpool had lost the bid in an auction the night before. So had Vanderpool decided to take another run at buying the painting away from Drake? Could he have brought someone else in with him whom Megan hadn't seen? Paul made a note to himself to talk with both men's secretaries.

"I also did some checking," Maria's voice interrupted his thoughts.

"And?"

"Now this is just my supposition, but I don't think the teenage daughter is Vanderpool's."

Paul set his mug down. "What?"

"The Vanderpools have a teenager. She attends a school in Connecticut. I had the school send over her file. Good grades, well liked but she looks nothing like her father and very little like the mother. Very dark hair, olive skin with hazel eyes. Her mother's eyes."

As he pictured the big Nordic-looking Vanderpool, Paul's curiosity was piqued. "Maybe they adopted."

"From someone with the same eye shape and coloring as Mrs. Vanderpool?" Maria tore a piece off her sticky bun and popped it into her mouth.

"Could happen." Though the chances were slim.

But where in the puzzle did Megan McClain fit in?

Paul's cell phone rang. "Wallace," he answered.

"Hey, the medical examiner has something of interest," Andy said. "And the security video from McClain's building is available."

"On my way," Paul replied, and hung up. "Gotta go. Apparently the medical examiner has something of interest," Paul explained to Maria as he stood. "Thanks for the heads up. I'll follow through and see what comes of it."

Maria nodded and waved a goodbye. Paul stopped at the cashier and paid for both of their tabs before heading back out into the cold. Andy was waiting for him by the sedan. They climbed in and made their way through the pulsing beat of traffic to the medical examiner's office on First Avenue, a square concrete building with little curb appeal.

"Yes," he replied, though there was a hint of wariness in his voice. "Where are you?"

"I'm home now. But I need to head to the gallery soon."

"I'll meet you at the gallery in two hours. Will that work?"

She nodded. Then gave herself a little shake since he couldn't see her nod. "Yes. Two hours."

She hung up. She had two hours to figure out where she'd seen the scarf before.

At the gallery in a stack of unused photos boxed away in the workroom, Megan found what she was looking for. A photo from last spring's fund-raising art exhibit to benefit The Children's Hospital of New York.

In the background of one photo showcasing Mr. Sinclair and the artist, a woman stood facing the camera, her dark hair curling around her shoulders barely showing the green silk scarf at her throat. Megan remembered the exhibit and the woman, who had attended with her father, a big contributor to the hospital.

Megan searched through more photos and found another picture of the woman, her father and Mr. Sinclair. Uncertainty burned in her chest. Why would this woman want to frame Megan for murder?

Taking the photo from the workroom where she'd immediately gone upon arriving at the gallery, Megan went in search of her employer, since she was sure he'd know the identity of the woman.

After having the crime scene released by the police and open again, the gallery was quiet, with just a few patrons wandering through the colored rooms. Joanie smiled as Megan passed by the reception desk. As Megan ascended the stairs, she wondered where Lacy was. Usually, Lacy would come in to the workroom needing direction.

But not today.

In fact, as Megan thought on it, Lacy hadn't sought her direction the past few days. But then again, Megan had been distracted with her brothers in tow.

Megan stopped at Mr. Sinclair's closed door and knocked.

"Come in," he called out.

She opened the door and entered. Surprise flickered through her at the sight of Lacy and Mr. Sinclair hunched over the account books. Megan hadn't even noticed the books missing from their place in the records room. She chalked it up to being distracted, which kind of freaked her out. Normal people were easily distracted, not people with OCD. Maybe she was gaining some ground in conquering her illness.

Mr. Sinclair glanced up and smiled. Lacy kept her head down and ignored Megan.

"Megan, how are you today?"

"Good, sir," she said as she moved closer. Curiosity made her itch to know what they were reviewing.

Mr. Sinclair's gaze shifted toward the door. "No brothers today?"

"No. They've returned home," she replied.

"Ah." His gaze landed on the photo in her hand.

She held up the picture. "I was wondering if you could identify the woman in this photo."

Lacy finally looked up, her expression unreadable.

"Hey, Megan, we were just looking at the accounts for the fall exhibit and we've come across some discrepancies."

"What?" Discrepancies? She never made mistakes because she always triple-checked her balances. Megan moved around the desk to look at the ledgers. "What are you referring to?"

"There are pieces inventoried in the ledgers, but no record of sales, and the pieces are not in the warehouse," Lacy explained, her blue eyes holding a hint of accusation.

"That can't be!" Stunned by the implication in Lacy's words, Megan said, "I've kept meticulous records. The artwork must be in the warehouse if they haven't been sold or put out for display."

"The pieces aren't in the warehouse nor are they currently on display," Lacy insisted.

Reeling from this news, Megan tried to keep her voice from showing her upset. "We'll have to take an inventory of the warehouse. Maybe the pieces have been inadvertently moved."

Lacy exchanged a glance with her great-uncle. "I've been inventorying the warehouse for the past two days. There are three pieces of art missing."

Feeling like her legs would buckle any second,

Megan grabbed the desk to steady herself. "That can't be." She turned her gaze to Mr. Sinclair. His grim expression slammed into her like a fist. "You don't think I've stolen them, do you?"

"Frankly, Megan, I'm not sure what to think in light of all that has happened," he replied, his voice full of regret.

Megan couldn't believe her ears. "But you know me. You know I couldn't do this. I couldn't, wouldn't have stolen paintings, let alone have killed those men."

His grim expression sent ribbons of dread curling through her. He didn't know her. Not really. She'd never told him about her OCD. To him she was just super-organized and a germ freak. Acid burned in her stomach.

"I think it would be better, Megan, if you…take some time off until this is all settled," Mr. Sinclair stated.

His words rocketed to her brain and exploded. Take time off? Did he really mean… "You're firing me?"

The regret in his eyes spoke volumes. "No, I didn't say that. Just a layoff until everything settles. I'm sorry, Megan, but I can't jeopardize my business for you."

"How am I jeopardizing your business?" she asked, stunned by his pronouncement even as the headlines of the murders flashed in her mind. Of course she jeopardized the gallery's reputation. Of course he couldn't have her here. But knowing that didn't make accepting it any less painful.

"The police have been informed of the discrepancies," Lacy interjected, her voice consoling but firm. "It wouldn't behoove my great-uncle to keep a murderer and thief on staff."

But I'm innocent until proven guilty. Megan stared at Lacy and Mr. Sinclair as if she'd never seen either of them before. How could they believe that of her?

The gallery was all she had, all she ever wanted to do. If she didn't have her work, what would she do with herself?

The edges of the photo cut into her palm as her hand tightened around it.

Determination solidified in her heart. She'd clear her name and get her job back. What other option was there?

Adding some starch to her spine, she raised her chin and said, "When my name is cleared, will I have my job back?"

Mr. Sinclair nodded. "Of course, Megan. You're the best curator I've ever had."

Then why did he believe she'd done these awful things? She'd have to prove to him and to the police she was innocent. She had to take back control of her life.

She held out the photo. "Who is the woman in this picture?"

Mr. Sinclair stared at the image for a moment. "That's George Grieger's daughter, Carol."

"Thank you," she said, before turning on her heel and walking out of the office. She stumbled down the stairs and paused before turning the corner where she'd have to face Joanie. Wiping at the tears that welled in her eyes, she forced herself to stand tall and composed. She had work to do; there was no time for feeling sorry for herself.

Calmly, she walked to the reception desk where she opened the panel concealing the cupboard that housed her things.

"You're going out?" Joanie asked, her gaze curious.

"Yes. I have some things to take care of," Megan replied as she sprayed her boots and then slipped her feet out of her pumps and into the boots. She paused as it occurred to her she needed to tell Paul that she wouldn't be here when he arrived.

She dialed his cell number but for some reason the call failed. She tried twice more and both times the call wouldn't go through. Figuring her cell signal must not be strong enough, she pocketed her phone and decided to try again in a while. Besides, she had to find out all she could about Carol Grieger before she talked with Paul. She wanted to have enough ammunition to point him in the direction of someone other than herself as the villain. Though why or how Carol Grieger had killed the two men, planted a painting in Megan's apartment and somehow cooked the gallery ledgers was beyond her.

Putting her coat on, Megan said to Joanie, "If a Detective Wallace shows up and asks for me, please tell him I'd had an errand to run and I'll call him later."

Walking into the frigid winter air, she pulled her coat tighter and tried to decide just how she was going to get to the main public library where she could research Carol Grieger. She started walking south, careful to keep herself from bumping the other pedestrians while she counted her steps beneath her breath.

The sounds of Manhattan filled her head. Horns, voices coming from every direction, the ringing of bells from the man dressed like Santa standing beside his red Salvation Army donation bucket and the merry music drifting out through doors opening and closing from the various shops and businesses. All the noise assaulted her already tightly wrung nerves.

She forced herself to keep moving. She had a name and a face to begin her own investigation with; she had to stay focused and in control.

As she came to the dark and dank stairwell of the green line subway station, she paused, her heart beating so rapidly in her chest she feared her ribs might crack. She watched as people of all colors and walks of life poured in and out of the opening that led to the underground railway system that could take her downtown in much less time than if she walked.

But could she do it? Could she bolster her courage and step down those stairs into the darkness beyond? Millions took the subway every day. She should be able to.

She stepped closer, holding herself tightly together as the throng of bodies around her thickened. Someone brushed past her shoulder. She recoiled. A man nearly rammed into her head-on before he sidestepped around her, his briefcase knocking against her leg.

She swallowed back the anxiety threatening to rob her of air. She took a step, looming near the subway entrance. People muttered expletives at being inconvenienced by her still body as she blocked their path.

No. She couldn't do it. She turned to walk away when she felt a hard shove from an open palm on her back. She stumbled forward, halfway down the stairs. A scream escaped as she lurched for the guard rail and clung to the nasty, sticky metal. She was bumped and jostled as she forced her way back to the top and burst out of the opening onto the sidewalk.

A shudder ripped through her as her lungs drew in big gulps of air. Her gaze searched the crowd, looking for a threat. No one in the sea of people seemed to be paying her any mind.

But she knew that someone had just tried to push her down the subway station stairs.

SEVEN

"Hello?"

"It's me," the caller said.

There was a sharp intake of breath. "What are you doing? You shouldn't call here. What if the police connect us?"

Impatience laced the caller's tone. "I'm using a public phone." Not far from where the caller had tried to push Megan down the subway station stairs. Only the shove hadn't been hard enough. Megan had caught herself too easily. Next time, Megan won't be so lucky.

"What do you want? You know the money hasn't been released yet and won't be for some time." There was a tremor of panic in the voice.

Frustration burned in the caller's belly. "Yes. I know. I need you to do something for me."

"Do?" The one word conveyed a big dose of wariness.

"Listen closely. I'm only going to explain this once."

* * *

Paul stared at the Sinclair Art Gallery's reception-ist in disbelief. "What do you mean Megan isn't here?"

Joanie shrugged her narrow shoulders. "She came in, talked with Mr. Sinclair and Lacy then left. She said she had something to take care of. She said to tell you she'd contact you later."

He didn't get it. Megan had sounded so…eager, bordering on desperate, to see him when she'd called earlier. And now she'd stood him up? It didn't make sense. She wasn't the type to make an appointment and then not show.

He moved away from the desk and used his cell phone to call the number from which Megan had called him earlier. She'd said she was at home then so he'd stored her number in his address book. The phone just rang. Frustrated, he snapped the phone closed and turned back to the receptionist.

"Are Mr. Sinclair and Lacy available?" Maybe they would know what errand Megan had run off to.

Joanie shook her head, her brown bobbed hair swaying. "No. Lacy's over at the warehouse doing more inventorying and Mr. Sinclair had to take his wife, Sylvia, to the doctor's. She's not doing so well these days."

"I didn't know Mrs. Sinclair was ill," Paul com-mented, and took out his notepad from the inside pocket of his leather bomber. Even though he was off duty today he always carried his notepad.

"She has rheumatoid arthritis, which makes it hard for her to get around, and then six weeks ago she fell and broke her ankle. I think they're taking the cast off today," Joanie explained.

"I see," he said, and scribbled down the information.

"Detective, did my alibi check out?" Joanie asked, her expression guileless.

He spared her a smile. "Yes." She'd been at her son's basketball game as she'd stated in her interview.

Joanie made a dramatic gesture with her hand to her forehead. "Whew. Just making sure."

Unfortunately, neither Joanie nor the guards had any useful information regarding the murders, the painting or Megan's connection to the victims. As of yet, Paul was keeping his conviction that Megan was being set up under wraps. He and Andy agreed that letting on that they were still looking for the true suspect might further endanger Megan's life. They hoped that if the real murderer relaxed in the knowledge that Megan was taking the fall, the person would slip up and reveal themselves.

Focusing on his task at hand, he asked, "Do you know Megan's cell-phone number?" He had it in his official report but not on his person.

"Yes." Joanie regarded him with a speculative stare. "Are you asking in an official capacity?"

As opposed to a man wanting an attractive woman's phone number? He could hear the unspoken question swirling around him. The answer was a little of both, but he wasn't going to share that with Joanie. "She's a suspect in a murder investigation," he stated, infusing authority into his tone.

Her eyes widened. "Right. Let me find it."

While she scurried about the desk, looking for Megan's number, Paul assessed the progress he and Andy had made in the past two days. The bartender at Figaro's couldn't say for sure that either of the two women whose pictures they'd shown him—Lacy Knight or Jasmine Oliphant—was the woman who'd talked with Sinclair the night of the murders.

Paul had arranged an interview with Mrs. Drake for Monday morning. Mrs. Vanderpool had gone into seclusion, and her lawyer was running interference.

And interviews with Lacy Knight's parents' neighbors had been fruitless. Apparently Tuesday nights were a big night for not being home.

"Here you go." Joanie offered him a scrap of paper with Megan's cell number scrawled across it.

"Thank you." Paul took the paper and left the gallery. On the street he called Megan. Her voice mail picked up.

Dread and apprehension slithered down his spine. There was no reason to believe she was in trouble.

But he still couldn't shake the feeling that something was wrong.

Paul started walking, not even sure where he was going. He just needed to move, to work off the anxiety growing in his gut.

Where was Megan? Manhattan was a big place to

search when he had no idea where to begin. He only hoped his gut was wrong and she was okay.

"Don't you think it could have just been some overeager commuter?" Dr. Miller adjusted his glasses on his thin face. "The subway entrances are crowded with people shoving to come and go."

Megan held on to her patience even as her certainty wavered. After her scare at the subway entrance, she'd immediately headed to the one place she felt safe. Dr. Miller's office. "I felt a hand on my back." But she supposed it could have been just someone trying to get past her. At the time she'd been so sure.

"It was brave of you to consider the subway system at such a stressful time," Dr. Miller commented. "You seem to be handling this whole ordeal quite well. I'm proud of the progress we've made."

Megan was proud, too. When she'd first started seeing the psychologist not long after she'd arrived in New York, the mere idea of the subway had made her break out in hives.

She thought about the past few days and realized how much she had matured over the years away from her family. Away from her mother's smothering love.

"Tell me about this detective." Dr. Miller's gaze pinned her to her chair.

Startled, she asked, "What do you mean?"

A small smile played at the corners of his mouth. "You've mentioned Detective Wallace in almost every sentence as you related the events of the past few days. I assume he has some special meaning to you."

She swallowed hard, trying to catalog her feelings and her thoughts, but failing. "A special meaning? Okay, maybe. Is that so bad?"

"Bad? No, on the contrary. I think you developing feelings for someone is a very good sign. You know people who suffer with OCD can have healthy relationships. There's no reason you shouldn't explore your feelings for this man."

Anxiety twisted in her chest. "But what if he finds out about my illness and…" She turned to stare at the full bookshelves.

"And what, Megan? What is it you fear?"

"Everything," she said dryly.

"What specifically with this man?"

She sighed. "That he'll think I'm a freak just like everyone else does."

"I don't think you're a freak," he said.

"That's because I pay you," she shot back.

He gave her a chiding look. "God doesn't think you're a freak."

She clung to that knowledge. "I know."

"So why not give this man a chance? Take a risk?" Dr. Miller's voice held encouragement.

"I don't know if I can," she replied, and glanced at the clock, relieved to see the hour he'd given her was up. She wasn't liking the direction the conversation was taking. "Oh, look, it's been an hour."

His expression told her he knew what she was doing. Avoiding.

She rose from the leather chair and grabbed her coat. "Thank you, Dr. Miller, for squeezing me in so quickly."

He walked her to the office door. "You know you can call anytime. And if you really feel that someone deliberately tried to push you down the subway stairs, you should tell this detective."

"No, you're right. I'm just being paranoid. It's like you said, it was crowded and people were trying to get past me. I'll see you next week," she said, and hurried to the elevator.

As she waited for the doors to open she reflected on how when she'd first moved to New York she'd had the hardest time with elevators. Her heart would race, her throat would constrict until she thought she'd faint. But now, elevators were no sweat.

She rode the elevator to the first floor. Her gaze panned the crowded lobby as men and women in business attire moved about their day. A bicycle messenger rode his bike onto the marble foyer and the attendant at the information desk chided him for leaving tire marks. A man in a leather jacket stood propped against the wall reading a newspaper. A woman with a stroller nudged past Megan and headed outside.

A buzzing drew Megan's attention. She pulled her cell phone out and it buzzed in her hand, alerting her she had a voice mail. Quickly she checked the message. Paul's voice filled her head. He sounded concerned and wanted her to call him back as soon as possible.

She dialed Paul's number. He answered on the first ring. "Megan?"

"Yes. Hey, I'm sorry about earlier," she said quickly, realizing she'd forgotten to try his cell again.

"Are you okay? Where are you? What did you need to see me about?"

"Whoa, one question at a time. I'm okay. I'm in midtown, near Rockefeller Center." She'd planned to tell him about the scarf but now she wasn't ready. She had no proof it was Carol Grieger's even if it did look like the one in the picture. Megan could have easily bought one and forgotten about it. Megan would find out more information first before getting Paul involved. The last thing she wanted to do was appear crazy with wild accusations based on a random scarf.

"I can be there in ten minutes," he stated.

She blinked. "Okay. Let's meet in front of the ice rink near the tree."

"I'll see you in few." He hung up.

Megan pocketed her phone and, with a light step, headed toward Rockefeller Center's ice arena.

There she was. Megan. Standing near the base of the eighty-foot-tall Norway spruce framed by thousands of tiny multicolored lights that reflected off her dark, shiny hair to create a kaleidoscope aura around her.

Paul's heart heaved a sigh of relief.

He chose not to look closely at the emotions running through him as he weaved his way through the crowds to her side. Nor did he stop himself from pulling her into his arms.

"You scared me." The words burst forth before he could censor them. He took a deep breath and contained the next words that trembled on his tongue, *don't do it again.*

She mumbled something into his chest. He eased back and drank in the surprise in her bright eyes and the shy smile on her well-formed lips.

"I'm sorry. I didn't mean to upset you. I've never had anyone worry about my whereabouts besides my brothers. I just didn't think…" she said in a rush.

Didn't think he cared? No, he didn't suppose she knew how he felt, especially since he wasn't too sure yet, either. He tried to brush off his emotions and actions as nothing more than his need to fulfill his promise to her brother that he'd keep an eye on her. He took his responsibility seriously. "You sounded so desperate this morning, I was…"

Afraid. Terrified. Sure that something bad had happened to her. He couldn't say any of that. He jammed his hands into his pockets.

She studied him for a moment. "You were really worried."

He made a noise in his throat, half growl, half scoff. "What did you need to see me about?"

Her gaze shifted away to the skaters twirling on

the ice. Turning back to him, her expression pensive, she said, "I lost my job today. Laid off for now is what he said. At least until after my name is cleared."

He'd figured that was coming and had been surprised that Sinclair hadn't fired her the first day after the murders and now that two more paintings had disappeared...Sinclair had a business to run. "I'm sorry."

Her beseeching gaze tore at him. "You don't really think I could have murdered those two men, do you? Or stolen the other paintings?"

His instincts told him she was being set up, but deceit had many faces. Was Megan's one of them? Deciding it would be better to gain her trust, so he could keep an eye on her, he went with his gut. "No, I don't," he said, praying he was right.

Relief swept her features and left a pleased smile on her face. "Good." She turned back to watch the skater. "I've never skated here, have you?"

"No." On impulse he grabbed her hand and pulled her toward the box office. "Let's skate right now."

"Aren't you on duty?" she asked, her voice just a notch higher than before.

"I'm off today. Come on," he said, and tugged her hand.

"Oh, I couldn't," she protested, though she hurried to keep up.

"Do you have somewhere you have to be?" he asked as they stopped before the ticket counter.

"No," she replied.

"Then there's no reason not to. Even if you've

never skated, I can teach you the basics." He bought two tickets then led her to the skate rental counter. "What size shoe are you?"

"Eight," she supplied.

Her eyes were wide and her face a bit pale. She looked like she could blow chunks any moment. Paul told the guy their shoe sizes and took the skates offered. "Oh, hey, do you have any antibacterial spray?" Paul asked the man.

A moment later, spray can in hand, Paul led Megan to a bench and handed her the can.

Her stunned smile made his heart jump.

"That was so thoughtful," she said, and sprayed the inside of each skate before taking her own shoes off and putting her feet into the skates. By the time she was laced up, Paul had his skates on and was anxious to get out on the ice.

He held out his hand. "Ready?"

Her warm palm settled over his. "Yes."

As they stepped onto the ice, Megan said, "I haven't done this since I was little."

She wobbled and clung to Paul's arm. So at least she wasn't a total novice. "Steady now," he said. He'd played ice hockey in high school. "It's like riding a bike. Once you get your balance you'll be fine."

"You'll catch me if I fall?" she asked, her face full of concentration as she sought to find her equilibrium.

Warmth curled around his heart. "Yes, I'll catch you."

For the next two hours they laughed and twirled

and glided around the arena, dodging other skaters while trying to stay close to each other. Paul couldn't remember the last time he'd felt as carefree as he skated alongside Megan, his hand at her back, ready to catch her if she stumbled. And the pure joy on her face filled his heart with exhilarating pleasure.

When they'd skated themselves out, they headed back to the bench where they changed from the skates back to their street shoes.

"That was fabulous," Megan exclaimed as they left the ice rink and headed back toward the street.

"It was." Paul didn't want the day to end. He touched her elbow. "I'm famished after all that exercise. Let's go to the Sea Grill for an early dinner."

Uncertainty entered her gaze. "Eat out?"

Was she so germophobic she couldn't eat restaurant food? He tried to reassure her. "It's a five-star restaurant, meeting every possible standard the food industry has for cleanliness, with excellent food and service. And it's right here."

A smile trembled over her lips, belying the hesitation in her blue eyes. "I guess it would be okay."

He took her hand. "Trust me, you'll love it."

"I do trust you," she said softly.

Paul couldn't deny how much her words meant to him.

Nor could he deny how much he was coming to care for this beautiful, soft-spoken woman.

He led her through the thrumming hodgepodge of visitors at Rockefeller Center to the glass-enclosed elevator that whisked them below street level to the famed Sea Grill.

Though they didn't have reservations, the hour was early enough that they were seated right away at a table in the center of the room where they had a clear view of the gold-gilded statue of Prometheus and of the skaters exhibiting various levels of skill as they skated around the ice.

Christmas music played softly in the background. Red-bowed green wreaths adorned the wood-paneled walls and tiny lights were draped across the rectangular fountains, the glow reflecting in the flowing water. The ambience was a mixture of serenity, playfulness and grandeur, but more comfortable than posh.

A basket of warm cheese-drizzled toast was set in the middle of the small round table. Water goblets were filled. Paul liked the way Megan's gaze took everything in, clearly revealing she'd never dined in the restaurant before.

He pointed out some of the dishes he preferred on the menu. She chose the sea bass while he ordered the scallops.

"This is wonderful," she said as they waited for their dinner. "Thank you for suggesting it."

"Good food is one of my vices," he replied.

She eyed him. "You don't look like food is a passion."

He chuckled. "I work out as often as my schedule allows."

"Ah." She grinned and sipped from her water. "I jump rope."

No wonder she had such a trim figure. "Where?"

"In my apartment," she replied with a grin.

"Your downstairs neighbor doesn't mind?"

She shrugged. "I've never heard a complaint."

"Nice." He took a piece of cheese toast and put it on his plate. "What do you have planned for the weekend?"

"Sleeping in. Doing some Christmas shopping and church on Sunday. And you?"

"I'm on tomorrow, but have no plans for Sunday except to watch football," he replied, thinking how lame that sounded. Home alone with just the television. "Though my sister and niece might come down after church to shop, so I might hang with them."

"Do you *not* go to church then?" she asked, her gaze inquiring but not judgmental.

He shook his head. "Not since I left home."

She raised her eyebrows. "So you did at one time. Why did you stop?"

He shrugged. "I don't know. It's not that I don't believe in God. I know He exists and I'm pretty sure He has saved my sorry hide on many occasions, but I'm a realist. I have a hard time putting faith in a God who would allow so much evil in the world."

"But the world is full of sin, and that is where the evil comes from," she argued, her gaze beseechingly earnest. "If God didn't give humans free will, the freedom to decide how we act and the ability to make moral choices, we'd all be puppets on a string, little more than robots without a soul."

"So you're saying evil is necessary?"

"No, I'm saying evil is a part of our world derived from the hearts of humans. And faith is not designed to make everything tidy and sensible. Because the world isn't tidy and sensible."

Though he had a feeling she wished the world were tidy and sensible. "Then what is it for?"

"To deepen our relationship with God our creator. He longs for us to choose Him, but He leaves the choice to us."

He wasn't sure how to respond as he processed through her words. He agreed that evil lurked in the hearts of humanity, but he had to choose a relationship with God. What did that mean?

Thankfully, the waiter arrived with their meal and the conversation turned to less controversial and more comfortable topics such as movies, books and sports.

"You're a baseball fan?" he asked, not expecting her to be a sports person.

"You bet. I couldn't have grown up with three athletic brothers without some of it rubbing off," she commented between bites.

"Maybe this spring we could catch a Yankees game," he said, and then realized the suggestion in his words, that they would still be in contact with one another. That she wouldn't be in jail.

She gave him a shy, pleased smile. "I'd like that."

"I would, too," he said, holding her gaze, and not for one second regretting the implication that he wanted to see her again.

"But I have to tell you, I'm a Red Sox fan all the way."

He chuckled. "Of course you are, being from Boston and all."

An idea popped to mind. "Would you be interested in seeing a Broadway play on Sunday afternoon? I was just thinking I could get tickets for my sister and my niece. And if you'd like, for us."

Her eyes lit up with delight. "That would be great. How could you get tickets on such short notice?"

"I have a friend who can get them," he said.

"I'd really like that," she repeated with a warm smile.

He felt like a giddy teen as he returned her smile. But a dark thought intruded on his happiness. What if his instincts were wrong?

EIGHT

Megan couldn't remember a time in her adulthood when she'd felt so happy and carefree. Spending the afternoon skating with Paul had taken her mind off the murders and made her feel normal. She so longed to be normal, to live like everyone else without the constant anxiety that threatened to rob her of control.

She'd made a big stride today by eating in a restaurant. The service had been exceptional and the food divine. Once she got over the thought of eating with silverware and off plates that others had touched, she'd done well and enjoyed the experience.

But as Paul hailed a taxi, the anxiety stirred to life within her once again, making her palms sweat inside her gloves. Normal people rode in cabs. Nothing bad happened to them. At least not usually. And she had to admit it was too cold outside to walk back to her apartment.

When the cab pulled to the curb and Paul opened the door, she forced herself to stay calm and climb in. She shuddered as she sat stiffly on the vinyl bench seat.

Paul climbed in and sat beside her. He gave her address to the driver.

Staring straight ahead, she tried to keep the panic at bay. She could do this. She had to. Letting Paul see her illness wasn't acceptable, regardless of what Dr. Miller said. She wouldn't risk having Paul look at her as if she were some freak. She could only nod at his attempts at conversation as she grew increasingly warm. She took off her gloves, shoved them into her coat pocket and folded her hands in her lap.

At her building, she practically jumped out of the taxi. If Paul noticed her anxiousness he didn't comment. He told the taxi to wait, which she figured meant he wasn't walking her inside. Last time he had, they'd found the painting and he'd had to arrest her. She pushed away the bad memory.

Paul took her bare hand. She stared at the way his palm fit over hers so perfectly and marveled at the warmth sluicing up her arm.

"I'll call and let you know if I can get the tickets for Sunday," he said.

"That'd be great," she answered, her gaze lifting to his at the realization that she wasn't in the least freaked by the skin-to-skin contact. In fact, she liked the feel of his strong hand against hers.

There was a distance in his eyes that hadn't been there before. Confusion ran through her mind. Had she said or done something to make him regret his offer?

He leaned close. Her heart rammed against her ribs in anticipation of a kiss. She'd only ever been kissed once. By Bobbie Connelly in the third grade. But that was before her illness. After that she hadn't let anyone get close.

Paul's lips gently touched her cheek before he straightened and turned away. Disappointment coursed over her in waves as he turned her around and pointed her toward the door.

With measured steps she retreated to the safety of the building and, as she waited for the elevator, she watched Paul's taxi drive away. Inside her apartment she tried to banish her worry over Paul.

No matter how much she enjoyed spending time with him, a relationship between them would never work if she didn't clear her name. Perhaps that was the distance she'd noticed before he'd left her at the door to the building. He'd remembered who and what she was suspected of. A pain deep in her soul cried at the thought that he had doubts of her innocence. Had his words earlier this evening, when she'd asked if he thought her guilty and he'd said no, been a lie? Was he playing her? Waiting for her to slip up?

Taking the green silk scarf from her coat pocket, she fingered the material. She sat for the longest time, trying to remember ever purchasing the scarf. She was pretty certain she hadn't. And since she wanted to take control of her situation, she decided she'd find out what she could about the woman in the photo who wore a scarf like the one in Megan's hand.

She fired up her laptop and as soon as the machine was up and running, she went to her browser and began searching the Web for Carol Grieger, not really expecting there to be anything.

Ten minutes later, she stared in dumbfounded disbelief at a society-page news article in which Carol Grieger-Drake and her husband Thomas Drake were christening a yacht in Sag Harbor.

Megan tried to understand what this meant. How had Carol Grieger-Drake's scarf gotten into Megan's apartment? If it was her scarf?

The questions bombarded Megan's mind, but no answers were forthcoming.

She should tell Paul what she found out. But would he think she was grasping at straws?

She had to take control of her life and that meant she'd go ask Mrs. Carol Grieger-Drake if she was missing a scarf.

Megan left her apartment on foot, bundled for the December cold. Though it was Saturday, traffic was still heavy as she made her way uptown and over toward Central Park. She had Carol Grieger-Drake's scarf in her pocket, as well as the photo from the gallery event and her head full of questions.

As she hoofed it through the park, she had the strangest sensation of being watched. She abruptly halted and swung around, panic surging.

"Hey," a jogger yelped as he nearly collided with her.

"Sorry," she muttered as the man deftly sidestepped her to continue on his way.

Megan's gaze searched the roadway, blocked off

as it always was on the weekends so New Yorkers could enjoy the park with ease and without worry of car traffic.

She didn't see anyone particularly interested in her. A woman, dressed in a puffy down jacket, pushed a baby carriage with a child so bundled that the baby's face was barely visible. An elderly couple, in their woolen coats, walked at a brisk pace. A man leaned on the guard rail surrounding the grass and smoked a cigarette.

You're just being paranoid, she told herself. But she still hurried. She veered off Park Drive and took one of the footpaths. The foot traffic died down and soon she found herself alone walking through the wonderland of snow-covered boulders and stretches of lawn that were always crowded in the summer months but that were now desolate.

She heard a noise and whipped around. Nothing was there. Must have been a bird or a squirrel.

Quickening her pace, she veered off onto another path that headed west. She'd memorized Carol Grieger-Drake's address. A posh one to be sure in the Central Park West neighborhood. Up ahead the path diverged to two walkways. One led through a shadowy tunnel but came out close to the roadway near the Drake residence and the other bent to the right to take a more cumbersome route.

Neither course appealed. She was becoming winded as it was and didn't relish the longer path. But as she stared into the shadows of the tunnel, a tunnel she'd traversed many times during warmer months, fear slithered up her spine, making her feel weak-kneed and vulnerable. She glanced over her shoulder to assure herself she wasn't being followed.

Every second she stood in indecision she grew colder, the sweat she'd worked up now making her itch.

Be brave, she told herself. Take the short route. You can do it. Just go!

She forced herself to take a step and then another until she was practically running through the tunnel. Her footsteps echoed off the stone walls. Her snow boots splashed in various puddles. She hit a patch of ice and her feet slipped out from under her. For a moment her arms cartwheeled in the air, then she was falling. She landed on the hard paved path with a jarring thud to her backside.

From somewhere behind her in the tunnel came a splash and the echoing sounds of footsteps.

Paul and Andy arrived at Carol Grieger-Drake's Central Park West apartment ten minutes prior to the appointed time. The thirty-six-floor white-brick high-rise had replaced the tennis courts of the adjacent Dakota in 1964, though to Paul the new building wasn't nearly as architecturally distinguishable as the famed Dakota.

Paul stopped outside the glass-enclosed lobby to talk with the doorman, while Andy went into the lobby to talk with the concierge. The doorman gave a glowing report of Mrs. Drake, but not so much of Mr. Drake.

"He was a cranky one," Eddie, the doorman, commented. His livery uniform was pressed and obviously worn with pride. A braided cap covered his balding head. "I sure didn't like seeing Mrs. D treated so shabbily."

"What do you mean?" Paul asked as he wrote down the information from Eddie.

"Mr. Drake was just always barking at her, if they were late, even when she'd be in the lobby waiting on him to come home from his office." Eddie shook his head, his brown eyes disapproving. "Rush, rush, rush. Mr. Drake was always in a hurry. I think Mrs. D doesn't like the city much. Now that Mr. Drake is gone, she's moving permanently to their home in Sag Harbor."

"I understand they have two grown sons. They ever come around?" Paul asked.

"The younger one's off at some high-priced college in the Midwest. He comes around on breaks. The older one lives in France. I haven't seen him since he was about twenty."

"Thanks, Eddie, you've been a help," Paul stated as he moved inside. Andy was waiting by the elevators. They compared notes and both of the building's employees had the same thing to say about Mr. and Mrs. Drake. Paul wondered if the privileged residents realized how much the building's employees gleaned of the tenants' lives.

They took the elevator to the apartment on the thirtieth floor. Paul's knock was answered quickly by a thin, glamorous woman who Paul assumed to be Mrs.

Drake. Her brown hair had been swept up and back in some sort of fancy twist. Pearls adorned her earlobes and encircled her slender neck. Her cream-colored cashmere sweater, pressed navy slacks and loafers made Paul wonder if she were headed out to sea.

"Detectives, please come in." Mrs. Drake motioned them into the elegant entry gallery.

The stark white walls were lined with paintings and the herringbone hardwood floors shined beneath the overhead crystal chandelier. Mrs. Drake led the way to a square living room sporting black leather furnishings with a wondrous wall of windows giving a dramatic view of Central Park.

A separate dining area sported a dark wood dining set with high-back chairs. Beyond the dining room, Paul glimpsed the black granite countertops of the eat-in kitchen and the stainless-steel appliances that also reflected a high polish.

"Daddy said you had some more questions?" Mrs. Drake prompted.

"Yes, thank you for seeing us." Paul took out his notepad. "You said your husband was at a business dinner the night he was killed."

"That is correct," she said as she sat on the leather couch and crossed her ankles while laying her hands on her knee. Her face remained expressionless.

"Do you know who this business dinner was with?" Paul asked, as his gaze searched for any visible signs of abuse. If there had been any, they were now gone, just as the abuser was now gone.

"No. As I told your chief, my husband didn't involve me in his business dealings."

"Do you know why your husband wanted the Wahlberer painting?" Andy asked.

"No."

"Did you ever hear your husband speak of Megan McClain?" Paul asked, almost afraid of the answer.

"No. I hadn't heard of the woman until the story of her arrest appeared in the papers," she replied primly.

"So you have no idea why she would want to kill your husband?" Andy inquired, his tone casual but his eyes sharp.

She blinked and shifted her gaze toward the wall of windows. "No."

Paul exchanged a glance with Andy. Was the woman lying or really bereaved? "Have you and your husband bought artwork from the Sinclair Gallery before?"

She shook her head.

"Do you know of anyone who would have wanted your husband dead?" Paul asked.

"No." Her dark blue eyes bored into him.

"Did you ever hear your husband speak of a Mr. Henry Vanderpool?"

She shook her head emphatically. "No."

Her cardboard, stoic answers were beginning to bug Paul. Maria had said her eyes were cold. Paul could see that coldness in Mrs. Drake's controlled demeanor. But there was something she was holding back, Paul could sense it. Was it the abuse? "Did your husband abuse you?"

She abruptly stood, her face a tight mask. "That is enough. This interview is over. You have my husband's murderer. Why are you asking me these questions?"

"I know this is hard, but please bear with us," Andy said soothingly.

Paul had hit a nerve. "If he was abusing you, anyone could understand wanting him dead."

"I don't know what you're talking about. You have that woman. She killed him," Mrs. Drake insisted, her voice rising a notch.

"Why would she have killed your husband?" Andy pressed.

"How should I know?" There was a tremble in her voice that betrayed her.

"Was your husband having an affair?" Paul probed, gauging her reaction.

"Get out. Now." She pointed her finger to the entryway.

Paul closed his notebook. "I heard you're leaving town."

"That would not be a good idea until this case is closed," Andy remarked.

"Out!" she screamed, no longer cold but definitely alarmed.

In the elevator, Paul said, "So what do you think she's hiding?"

There was a grim expression on Andy's face. "I don't know. But we better find out. We certainly rattled her cage. The chief is going to blow a gasket."

"No kidding."

They stepped out of the elevator and into the lobby. Andy nodded toward the front entrance. "Isn't that your girlfriend?"

Paul didn't have a girlfriend. Confused by his partner's statement, his gaze zeroed in on a dark-haired beauty standing on the other side of the glass revolving door, animatedly talking with Eddie the doorman.

Paul groaned. "What is she doing here?"

Megan ground her teeth in frustration as she argued with the behemoth doorman who blocked her entrance to see Mrs. Drake. He was as immovable as a boulder and just as big. And after having had the scare of her life in the park she wasn't in the mood for stubborn.

After her fall, the man who'd been in the tunnel tried to help her up, but she'd allowed fear to get the better of her and she'd jumped up and run. And run. Until she'd made it to the Mayfair Towers, winded and angry at her own foolishness. The man was probably just some Good Samaritan, not any-one sinister.

"Please, I'm just asking for five minutes of her time," Megan said again.

"Sorry, miss. Mrs. Drake gave strict instructions she was to have no unexpected visitors today," he repeated for the umpteenth time.

"But I'm sure she'll see me," Megan replied, and

pulled the green scarf from her pocket. "I have her scarf. I need to return it."

He held out his hand. "I'll make sure she receives it."

Clutching the wisp of material, Megan shook her head. "No. I have to ask her some questions."

The doorman crossed his arms over his chest. "Look, lady. The answer's no. You better move on before I call the cops."

"That won't be necessary," came a familiar voice to Megan's right.

"Paul! What are you doing here?" she asked as she stuffed the scarf back in her pocket.

"I'd like to ask you the same question," he stated, his sharp green eyes slicing through her.

"I have to see Mrs. Drake," she explained. "I have some questions for her."

From Megan's left, she heard a scoff. She glared at Paul's partner, who arched a dark eyebrow at her in return. She turned back to Paul. "I have to see her."

Paul took Megan by the arm and dragged her away from the prying ears of the doorman. "Do you know how bad this looks? You can't visit the widow of the man you're accused of murdering. Do you *want* to end up in jail?"

"No, of course not." She bit her lip. She knew how this looked, like she were some crazy person out to stalk Mrs. Drake. She had to gain control of the situation. The only way to do that was to confide in him. She held out the scarf. "I found this in my apartment."

"Okay." His gaze searched her face. "So?"

"*So*. It belongs to her. How did it get into my apartment?"

"How do you know it's hers?" he countered, his expression skeptical.

She untucked the photo of Mrs. Drake, her father and Mr. Sinclair at the gallery from her purse. "See, she's wearing it."

Paul took the picture and stared at it for a moment. "Was this photo taken in the gallery?"

"Yes. A fund-raising event last year." She pointed to the scarf at Mrs. Drake's neck. "This is the same scarf."

Paul took the scarf. "Where did you find it?"

"In the hall closet where we found the painting."

Paul nodded, and she breathed a sigh of relief.

"I'll go ask her about this," Paul said. "You head home."

"I'm coming with you to talk with her," she said.

He gave her an are-you-kidding-me look. "Uh, no. You are going home and staying out of this."

"But this is my life," she exclaimed, needing him to understand how much she had to lose.

"And you need to trust me to do my job," he replied.

"I do," she said quickly.

"Then go home and I will call you." His left eyebrow rose a fraction as if to challenge her to deny his request.

"I'll wait," she ground out in stubborn determination. She wouldn't be overprotected and coddled. Not by Paul.

He stared at her for a moment before he shook his

head. "Fine. You wait with Andy. And then we'll take you home."

"Fine," she shot back.

Paul went to talk with Andy before nodding to the doorman and entering the building.

Megan smiled at Andy, who just stared at her, his dark eyes assessing. She had the distinct impression that Paul's partner didn't share Paul's certainty that she was innocent.

She sent up a silent prayer for God to bring the truth to light.

Paul knocked on Mrs. Drake's door. A few moments later, the door swung open.

Mrs. Drake's midnight-blue eyes widened. "Detective? What now?"

"I'm sorry to bother you, but I just have a few more questions," Paul stated, and held out the photo. "Is this you?"

She flicked her gaze at the picture. "Of course it is."

"Do you still own this scarf?"

Her eyebrows rose. "Yes. It's in my closet. What is this about?"

"Would you mind getting it?"

"Why? What does my scarf have to do with anything?"

"A scarf like this was found at the scene of a crime," he replied.

The color drained from her face. "No. My scarf is here."

She turned on her loafer-clad heel and walked away. Paul followed as far as the living room. He stood gazing out at the winter wonderland of Central Park, the trees dusted with white powder and the world so peaceful, idyllic, like a Hallmark card. Only he knew the truth. Life out there and in here, where the appearance of serenity reigned, was messy and complicated.

Complicated with a capital *M* for Megan McClain. She complicated his world, his sense of how his life should be lived. He still couldn't believe she'd had the audacity to think she could just waltz up to Mrs. Drake, wave that scarf in her face and not be hauled off to jail for harassment. He admired her spunk even as he deplored how much trouble she could have gotten herself into.

When Mrs. Drake didn't return after several minutes, Paul headed in the direction she'd disappeared. He found her in a large bedroom, the majority of space taken up by a huge king-size four-poster mahogany bed. Mrs. Drake was at the matching dresser, flinging clothes out right and left.

"Mrs. Drake?"

She whirled around. "I can't find it. It must be at the dry cleaners."

No, it was in his pocket. "Do you have any idea how your scarf would have ended up in Megan McClain's apartment?"

Her eyes filled with stunned surprise. "No. No, I don't."

"Why did you lie to me earlier when you said you'd never been to the Sinclair Gallery?"

Her hand went to her throat, her slender fingers played with the pearls. "I didn't mean to lie. I don't remember that gallery. There have been so many. Thomas or my father are always dragging me to some function or another at one gallery, restaurant or ballroom. I can't keep them all straight. I don't enjoy it. It's their world, not mine."

"But you were born to that world," Paul remarked, thinking how much more vulnerable she appeared now than earlier.

She gave a bitter laugh. "Yes, I was born to it. Born to spend my years banished to boarding schools or camps because a child cramped my parents' social style. I met Thomas in college. He dragged me back to this life."

Her resentment was unmistakable. But was it motive enough for murder? And if so, how had she done it?

NINE

When Paul emerged from the building, Megan rushed to his side, leaving Andy standing alone. Her heart galloped in her chest, threatening to break free. "Well? What did she say? The scarf is hers, right?"

Grim-faced, Paul nodded. "It could be. She can't find hers."

Andy came forward. The two men exchanged a silent glance that they both seemed to understand. "I'll get the car," Andy said, and took off down the street.

Megan stared after Andy for a moment then turned to Paul. Disbelief and disappointment oozed through her. "So why aren't you arresting her? Taking her in for questioning?" she demanded. "She has to be involved in her husband's murder and in planting the painting in my apartment. How else could the scarf have gotten there?"

"This scarf proves nothing," Paul stated. "I'll give it to the crime lab to examine the material. Not that I think they'll find much, considering you moved it and have your DNA all over it," he said, and gave her a censuring look. "Next time, Megan, if you find anything that even resembles evidence, you don't touch it, you call me."

Frustration burrowed in deep. "Fine."

"And let's get one more thing straight," Paul said, his tone chiding. "You leave the investigating to me."

She frowned. He'd sounded like one of her brothers. "You don't think I'm capable?" Although he had a point. She wasn't a detective.

His expression softened as he brushed away a stray strand of hair that had blown across her cheek. "I think you're more than capable of getting yourself in trouble. I don't want anything bad to happen to you."

She swallowed back the tremor of sensation his touch and his words evoked. Her feelings for him were anything but sisterly as she stared into his eyes and wished he'd pull her within his warm embrace.

"Come on, let's get you home," he said as he stepped back and took her by the elbow.

She allowed him to lead her to the waiting sedan.

Once settled in the backseat she said, "I still don't understand why the scarf doesn't prove she was in my apartment."

"Megan, there are probably millions of women in the city who have that scarf," Paul said, his voice patient.

"But not me," she groused.

"Are you sure?"

She frowned. "Yes, I'm sure. I may have OCD, but

I don't have a memory problem." Though she had thought that very thing when she'd first found the scarf. But he didn't need to know that.

He stilled. "You have OCD?"

A hot flush of embarrassment burned her cheeks. "I do." She waited to see his revulsion or pity. All she saw was his handsome smile.

"That makes sense," he said.

"What does?"

"Some of your behaviors."

She tried to gauge what that meant and how he felt about her, but the car stopped in front of her building and Paul helped her out of the back. She longed to invite him up for tea so she could explore how learning of her OCD affected him and his feelings for her, but he was working and she clung to the hope that she would see him the next day. "Are we still good for tomorrow?" she asked, half dreading his answer.

He nodded. "Of course."

Heady anticipation chased away the disappointment of the afternoon and her insecurities.

He walked her to the entrance. "No more investigating on your own," he said firmly one last time before he left.

Needing reassurance that the scarf was indeed of value to her case, Megan called her lawyer, Hillary Gibberman, using the cell-phone number the lawyer had provided.

"Well, it certainly adds some interest. I'll contact

the police department Monday morning and see what I can find out. Megan, you really need to stay out of the police's way," Hillary said before hanging up.

Yeah, right. Everyone wanted her to be a good little girl and sit on her hands while the fate of her life was determined by others. Not a chance. She may have OCD but she would be in control of her life.

Come Monday she would figure out her next move.

Later that night as she sat curled on her couch with a cup of hot tea, and watching a sitcom, her phone rang.

"Hello?"

"Hi, it's me, Paul."

Like she wouldn't recognize the deep timbre of his voice or the shooting thrills screaming along her veins. "How are you?"

"Good. Hey, I just have a second, but I want to let you know. I couldn't get tickets to the play for tomorrow but I did for next Sunday. Are you still game?"

"Yes," she responded immediately, though a small voice inside her head whispered, *Unless I'm in jail.* She batted away that ugly thought.

"Great. My family will be joining us."

"You mean your sister and niece, right?"

He made a little noise in his throat before answering. "And her husband and my parents."

The prospect of meeting his family sent nervous chills sliding along her limbs. What would they think of her? The thought made her stomach churn. She had to clear her name before then, she told herself with determination. "Okay. Great. I'll see you then."

"Good night," Paul said before hanging up.

Megan sank back into the cushions of the couch. Oh, boy, what had she gotten herself into?

Sunday morning arrived with a new layer of snow covering the ground. Megan, bundled in her snow boots, wool coat and wide-brimmed, warm hat, went to the church not far from her apartment as she always did on Sunday mornings. She sat in the same pew in the same row. But her mind wasn't on the sermon but rather on the murders and the clues that didn't make sense.

The dead men, the painting, the scarf. How did they all connect? Who had entered the gallery while she was searching for Mr. Sinclair? Mrs. Drake?

A thought occurred to her. Where did Vanderpool fit in? He'd ranted that he'd been called and told the painting was his. Who'd called him?

That was a question she'd like to pursue. To-morrow she'd go visit Mrs. Vanderpool; hopefully Megan would have better luck seeing Mrs. Vander-pool than she had in trying to see Mrs. Drake.

Though maybe she should tell Paul, let him ask the questions. His concern for her safety touched her deeply. But she couldn't just sit idly by doing noth-ing. What was Dr. Miller always telling her? *The only way through your fears is to face them.*

Asking a few questions wouldn't put her in jeopardy. She'd be careful and not push too hard. But she had to do this. It was the only way she'd feel in control.

The congregation began clapping, indicating the end of the service and startling Megan out of her thoughts. Guilt for not paying attention made her cheeks heat.

Today looked to be a long, lonely day, she thought as she filed out of the church building and headed home. Though she could count on her mother and possibly one, if not all, of her brothers to call. It seemed as if one or another had called every night the past few days. They were worried about her and that made her feel loved, so she didn't begrudge them the call.

Once inside her apartment she kept herself busy with her online Christmas shopping, which actually took longer than she'd expected since now she had two sisters-in-law, a future sister-in-law and a nephew to buy for, as well as her three brothers and mother. After exhausting her credit card, she decided to search her apartment again for any more clues. She didn't find any.

It was late in the afternoon when she heard a knock on her front door. Her heart picked up speed. Maybe Paul had decided to visit.

But it wasn't Paul's face she saw through the peephole, but Lacy Knight's.

Megan opened the door, not sure how to feel about her uninvited guest. "Lacy, this is unexpected."

Lacy's smile bubbled. "I'm sorry. I just wanted to see how you were. My great-uncle and I just feel terrible about having to let you go. We miss you."

Megan blinked in surprise. She'd had the distinct impression that Lacy had somehow instigated the layoff. Megan had always felt that Lacy had wanted her job and that Lacy resented Megan, so hearing that she was missed was a welcomed sentiment. Megan must have been wrong about Lacy's feelings. "Please, come in."

The younger woman bounced into the apartment with the exuberance of someone five years Megan's junior. Though Megan couldn't remember ever having that much energy even at twenty-three. Lacy's tall black boots left smudged imprints in the carpet. Megan forced herself to ignore them as she took Lacy's coat and hung it up. "Would you like some tea or soda?"

Lacy waved a hand. "No, thank you. I can't stay that long. I just wanted to make sure you were okay. Keeping yourself busy?"

"Yes, actually I am."

A moment of silence stretched between them, making Megan feel awkward. "Would you like to sit down?" she offered as she moved to the couch.

Lacy plunked down in the overstuffed chair. "Nice place. Very close to work."

"Yes, it is. Close to work, I mean," Megan said. "I picked it for that reason."

Lacy's dark blond eyebrows rose inquiringly. "Really? How very thorough of you."

Was there a hint of sarcasm in her voice? Megan tried to explain. "Your uncle offered me the curator position while I was still in grad school. So I had time to plan out my move to New York."

"Ah. Very smart."

An awkward moment of silence passed. Megan rose. "Are you sure you wouldn't like some tea?"

Lacy smiled. "Actually, that would be lovely."

Conscious of Lacy now perusing her CD collection, Megan brewed a pot of decaf tea and brought two mugs to the coffee table.

"Nice eclectic body of work," Lacy stated as she resumed her seat in the overstuffed chair.

"I enjoy a wide variety of music," Megan replied as she poured the tea.

"Me, too." Lacy sniffed the rising steam. "Yum, this smells good." She tasted it. "Tastes even better. What is it?"

"White tea infused with peach and mango," Megan replied before lightly blowing on the hot liquid.

"I'll have to remember that." Lacy sipped for a moment. "My aunt had her cast taken off."

Megan had been worried when she'd heard of Mrs. Sinclair's fall. "I'm glad. I know wearing a cast must have been hard on her."

"Yes, it was. She's not used to being so inactive." Lacy jumped up. "May I use your restroom?"

"Sure. First door on the right."

Megan fidgeted with the lamb's wool throw that lay across the back of the couch. Having another guest in her house felt strange. First Paul, then her brothers, and now Lacy. Her world was expanding. And that could only be a good thing.

Dr. Miller had told her often that if she'd let people in, she'd be more content. She hadn't understood what he'd meant, because she'd thought she was content with her life the way it was, but now she was seeing how much richer life could be with relationships.

Lacy rejoined Megan but didn't sit. "Hey, this has been fun. But I've got to go. My parents are expecting me for dinner."

"Oh, sure." Megan retrieved Lacy's coat from the hall closet. "Thank you for stopping by. That was very thoughtful of you, Lacy."

Lacy beamed, her blue eyes twinkling. "You're welcome." She patted Megan's arm. "Don't worry, all of this nonsense will be over soon. Bye now."

Alone again, Megan couldn't help but take an antibacterial wipe to the fixtures in the bathroom. Germs were germs and Megan could only allow so much growth in herself at one time.

Later that evening as Megan readied herself for bed, she pondered Lacy's words. *All of this nonsense.* Megan wasn't sure murder and theft could be classified as nonsense, but at least Lacy wasn't calling her a murderess.

Megan went into the bathroom to brush her teeth. Only her toothbrush wasn't in its holder. It had been there this morning. She'd used it.

She searched the floor, thinking maybe it had fallen out of the holder, but it was nowhere in sight. She checked the garbage can. Empty.

She'd taken out the garbage this afternoon, so if her toothbrush had been in the bathroom can at that time, it was now in the building's main garbage. Oh, well. Thankfully, she kept a megapack of toothbrushes handy.

As she got out a new toothbrush, her thoughts turned to Paul and his invitation to join his family next Sunday for a play. Nervous ripples chased through her stomach. She'd have to buy a new outfit for such a momentous occasion. And maybe even new shoes.

But the thought that had her quaking in her slippers was what if Paul's family didn't approve of her?

Monday morning, Megan hoofed across Lexington to the gallery in search of an address for the Vanderpools because she couldn't find anything online as she had for the Drakes. She worried her lip, praying that her visit to the gallery would be welcomed.

With trepidation, she entered the gallery doors. Joanie gave a squeal and came out from behind the reception desk to give her a hug. "I didn't know when we'd see you again. Are you back to work?"

"Regretfully, not yet," Megan said with a stitch in her chest, thankful for Joanie's warm welcome. She really missed her job and, surprisingly, the people. "Could you do me a favor and look up an address?"

"Of course." Joanie resumed her spot behind the counter. "Who are we looking for?"

"I need Henry Vanderpool's address."

Joanie gave her a censuring, surprised looked. "Are you sure? Isn't he one of the… I mean, why?"

Megan stepped closer, hoping to plead her case. "I have to find out why he came to the gallery that night. He wasn't expected. My life is on the line here, I have to know why."

Joanie considered her for a moment. Then gave a nod. "It'll just take a sec."

As Megan waited, her gaze was drawn to the walls of the rooms she could see into. She frowned and moved into the red room. It was all wrong. Someone had rearranged the works of art. Paintings and sculptures that belonged elsewhere were in prominent view.

Heart pounding, Megan went from room to room; with each step her breathing quickened at the chaos on the walls. The symmetry and harmony she'd striven to maintain over the years in the gallery was completely lost. Now, colors clashed, styles competed for attention rather than complementing each other.

Megan hurried back to the front desk. "Joanie, what happened? Why are the rooms so…so discordant?"

Joanie heaved a sigh of repugnance. "I tried to tell her, but she insisted on moving everything. She even brought in pieces from the warehouse that you'd stashed away for next spring's auction."

The muscles in Megan's neck tightened with agitation. Lacy. She'd done this. Hadn't she learned anything in the three years she'd worked under Megan? "Where is she?"

Joanie slid a piece a paper across the counter. "She's in the workroom."

Megan took the paper with the Vanderpool information. She noticed that Joanie had provided a city address as well as the location of the Vanderpool's Long Island home.

Clutching the paper in her hand, Megan stormed into the workroom and came to an abrupt halt as a shudder of pure dread ripped down her back. The once neat and orderly workbench was littered with tools and debris. Her stash of antibacterial wipes and cans of disinfectant spray were conspicuously missing. Paintings were randomly stacked against one wall.

Boxes with the white foam packing materials were randomly strewn across the floor; apparently after retrieving the contents, Lacy just left the boxes like obstacles in the path to the worktable where Lacy was bent over a framed work. Her backside bopped to some music only she could hear as she wiped at the gilded edges of the work's wood frame.

As every instinct inside screamed to bring order to the chaos, Megan approached. She touched Lacy's shoulder. The girl jumped as she swung around and yanked out the earbuds attached to an iPod hanging around her neck. "My stars, Megan, you almost gave me a heart attack. Do you always sneak up on people?"

"What are you doing? What is this?" Megan made

a sweeping gesture with the hand that held the Vanderpool information.

Lacy's gaze followed the fluttering paper before her eyes narrowed on Megan's face. "I'm working, as you can see. What are you doing here?"

Putting the slip of paper in her coat pocket, Megan replied, "I can't believe what you've done to the gallery."

Lacy arched an eyebrow. "You saw the rooms? I think they work. So does Uncle."

"They don't work. There's no flow, no symmetry," Megan countered. "And you've put out pieces that should be included in the spring auction."

Lacy shrugged. "We'll get new pieces. I just didn't see the point of having such fine work not out on display."

"The artists are expecting their work to be at the auction, not on the walls," Megan exclaimed, thinking how much of a headache it would be explaining to the artists what Lacy had done.

"Don't worry. I've got it all covered. It is *my* job now, you know."

The smugness in Lacy's voice stung like a slap to the face. "Only temporarily," she reminded the younger woman.

Lacy's mouth curled up but the smile didn't reach her eyes. "Of course."

A violent rage coursed through Megan, scaring her back a step. For now she had to let the situation go. When she returned, she'd put to right what Lacy had undone. But first, Megan had to clear her name so she could resume her life.

Without another word, Megan spun on her heel and walked out of the gallery. Anger beat such a heavy tune in her mind that she was hardly aware that she'd hailed a taxi until she was bumping along on the leather seat.

Surprise gave way to a satisfying sense of accomplishment. She'd actually hailed a cab and was on her way to Sutton Place where the Vanderpool's had a home on the East Side near the river. She was getting better.

The taxi stopped in front of a three-story townhome near a communal garden. As Megan stepped from the car, she felt as if somehow during the twenty-minute taxi ride, she'd been transported out of Manhattan to this charming residential enclave that almost looked like a movie set.

She checked the addresses and then resolutely walked to the door of the three-story private townhome. She knocked on the large ornately carved wooden door.

A few moments later the door opened. A strikingly beautiful teenage girl of about sixteen stared at Megan. She had dark, tightly curled hair and olive skin, with the most amazing hazel eyes. "Can I help you?" the girl asked.

"Is Mrs. Vanderpool home?"

The girl shook her head. "No, she's at the house in Water Mill. Was there something you needed?"

"Are you her daughter?" Megan asked, wondering why she hadn't found anything about the Vanderpools' child. Especially one who looked nothing like her father. She must favor her mother.

The only information she had found on the Internet had pertained to the corporation that Mr. Vanderpool had been the CEO of. There had been no pictures of his family. No mention of them that she could find.

Had Mrs. Vanderpool been married before? That would explain why the child looked nothing like Mr. Vanderpool.

The girl's gaze turned wary. "Yes. I'm Grace."

"I know this must be a difficult time with the death of your father, but could I ask you some questions?"

"Are you a reporter? Mom said I shouldn't answer any questions. Dad didn't want our lives to be public, and neither does my mom," Grace replied as she started to shut the door.

"No, I'm not with the press. I work at the art gallery," Megan said, hoping she wouldn't have to tell this girl that Megan was the one accused of killing her father.

She stopped closing the door. "Oh. That's where he was killed."

Megan nodded. "Yes. We're all terribly sorry for your loss. But your father had come there that night to buy a painting. Do you know anything about that?"

Grace's mouth twisted. "Yeah, Dad liked art. Come in, you can see his collection."

Grateful for the invitation, yet surprised by the girl's trust, Megan stepped inside. The entry was a beautiful shade of buttercup-yellow with wrought-iron wall sconces, casting a warming glow to the white-oak floors. Megan followed Grace through the posh, yet lived-in-looking main room, which had a door leading to an immaculately landscaped terrace.

Grace entered a darkened room and flipped on the light just as Megan stepped inside. Megan stared in surprise at the many valuable pieces of artwork surrounding her: paintings, sketches, sculptures and blown glass, showcased in large display cabinets. The collection was amazing.

"Wow, this is fabulous," Megan said with awe in her voice.

"My father's passion," Grace stated, with just a hint of bitterness in her voice.

Megan regarded the young girl. "Not your mother's?"

Grace gave a negative shake of her head. "No. In fact, I bet if you talk with Mom, she'd be willing to sell all of this plus the stuff at the other house."

"There are a lot things I'd like to talk to her about," Megan said, giving the girl her full attention. "Were you here the night your father died?"

"No. I was at my boarding school. I'm returning there this afternoon," she replied, and left the room.

"Will you return for Christmas?" Megan asked, sure that the girl's mother would want her child with her at such an emotional time.

Hurt flashed in the young girl's eyes. "On Christmas Eve and then return again the day after."

Aching for Grace, Megan trailed along behind her to the living room, where the girl picked up a soda can sitting on the glass coffee table. Gesturing with the can, she asked, "Do you want something to drink?"

"No, thank you." A sadness that this child was alone seeped into Megan. "Do you enjoy boarding school?"

Grace shrugged as she flopped onto the leather sofa. "It's okay. I think my mom liked it more than I do."

"What's the name of the school?"

"Covington's Academy, in Farmington, Connecticut."

"Did your parents grow up in Connecticut?"

Grace rolled her eyes. "Mom's family is from Connecticut but Dad was raised in the Midwest. Came East to *be* someone."

"Ah. Did they meet in college then?" Megan asked.

"Yes. At Columbia. But Mom never finished because they got married," Grace replied.

From the tone of her voice, Megan guessed the young Grace didn't plan on making that choice. "You must miss your family while you're at school."

Grace shrugged one shoulder. "Not really. We've never been close. You see, my dad wasn't my biological father."

"Oh." Megan detected the hurt underneath the matter-of-fact way Grace delivered the information. Megan understood the heartache of growing up without a father, but what Grace experienced was worse in a way. To have a father but not be close would be very painful.

A knock at the door echoed through the high-ceilinged home.

Grace made a scoffing noise. "What is this? Grand Central today?"

The girl left to answer the door and Megan wandered to the mantel where a very expensive bronze statue was the only decoration. Her gaze searched the walls, the top of the baby grand piano, the side tables. No family photos anywhere. Nothing that gave the room a personal touch.

From down the hall to the entryway Megan heard the door open and the familiar timbre of a certain homicide detective. Her senses went on alert and her first instinct was to hide because she knew he'd be furious when he discovered her there.

But she'd met and triumphed over too many fears this past week to let a little thing like being caught investigating by the handsome detective to send her back to wimpy cowardice.

She heard Grace invite Paul in. Megan faced the entryway with her chin held high. Andy stepped in first, his dark eyebrows rising nearly to his hairline. Then Paul stepped beside him, his gaze following his partner's to zero in on Megan.

His green eyes filled with fire as he came straight to her side and ground out, "What are you doing here?"

Her heart pounded so loud she was sure he heard it. "I was just leaving."

She tried to move away, but his hand snaked out and clamped on to her elbow. "I'll escort you out."

"Hey, do you know each other?" Grace said, her young face scrunched in confusion.

"Yes, we're old friends," Megan reassured her as Paul led her toward the entry. Megan dug in her heels and stopped their forward progress to say to Grace, "Thank you for your time."

She noticed Paul gesture to Andy over Megan's head. Andy deftly gained Grace's attention and began questioning her. Megan didn't have a chance to hear their conversation because Paul hauled her outside.

He released her and stared hard at her. "You shouldn't be here. This is so not okay."

Megan tried not to let his intimidating glare unnerve her as she tried to explain. "I just wanted to ask some questions. I remembered something Mr. Vanderpool said when he came to the gallery that night. I was hoping Mrs. Vanderpool could tell me why Mr. Vanderpool said he'd been told he could have the painting even after he was outbid by Mr. Drake."

"Let me get this straight," Paul said, his expression hard and incredulous. "You remembered something from the night of the murders and instead of calling me with this information, you chose to go snooping on your own, putting your life in danger."

She frowned, not liking how he made it sound. "I'm not in danger."

He arched one eyebrow. "Oh, really? So you don't

think someone trying to frame you for two murders qualifies for danger?"

Apprehension dried out her mouth. "Well, when you put it that way…"

"So you remembered Vanderpool saying he'd been told he could have the painting?"

"Yes," Megan replied. "That was why he showed up unexpectedly. If Mrs. Vanderpool doesn't know who called him maybe his secretary would?"

He nodded, a thoughtful look crossing his features. "I'll check that out. How did you get down here?" he asked.

Feeling pretty proud of herself for giving him another direction to search in and for her own bravery, she said, "Taxi."

He gave a single nod before marching to the corner of Fifty-seventh and hailing a yellow cab. He opened the door and motioned for her to enter. Knowing there was no use staying here since Grace hadn't been able to answer her question, Megan stalked down the block and climbed in.

Paul leaned in closer. "No more investigating or I'll haul you in for obstruction of justice and tampering with evidence."

Stunned disbelief that he would do such a thing rendered her speechless. Before she had a chance to gather her outrage, he slammed the door shut and tapped on the hood. The taxi shot forward. Megan twisted around to see Paul shaking his head as he walked back toward the Vanderpool's town house.

"Where did he tell you to take me?" she asked the driver, half expecting Paul had told him to take her to the police station.

The driver recited her apartment address.

She sat back, thinking over what Grace had said about her mother possibly wanting to sell her husband's art collection. It would be a boon for the Sinclair Gallery to handle the work. But she didn't work there anymore, at least not now, so she didn't feel that inclined to inform Lacy. But she could use the excuse of the artwork as a way to contact Mrs. Vanderpool.

That is, if Mrs. Vanderpool didn't realize that Megan was the accused killer.

Thus, clearing her name had to remain her number one priority, regardless of how angry she made Paul.

TEN

Megan had a plan. As soon as she arrived home, she fired up her computer and searched for the work addresses of both Drake and Vanderpool. As clandestinely as she could, she'd check out each place. Maybe someone who had worked closely with them, such as a secretary or assistant, might know something that could help Megan clear her name.

After finding the business addresses, she bundled back up and headed out. If she hurried she'd make it to both places before the offices closed for the evening.

Before leaving her building she stopped by her mailbox, since she'd forgotten to the day before. She wasn't sure if a court summons would come through the mail or if her lawyer would inform her of her arraignment date. She scanned through the bills and found a curious plain white envelope addressed to her with no return address. Her summons?

Putting the bills in her purse and tossing the junk in the lobby wastebasket, she moved to a planter near the decorative Christmas tree and tore open the seal on the letter.

The folded white sheet of paper slid out easily. The typed words virtually jumped at Megan.

Two men are dead. Stop asking questions or you'll be next.

Megan's breath caught. She glanced around. She was so very conspicuous. Her eyes widened as she reread the threatening note.

Realizing she was probably contaminating evidence by touching the paper, she carefully reinserted the sheet of plain white paper with its dreadful message back into the envelope, and then she rushed back to her apartment and called Paul on his cell phone, her fingers trembling.

He picked up on the fourth ring. "Wallace."

"Paul, it's Megan."

"What happened? You sound shaky."

"Okay, I'm admitting it. I put myself in danger."

"What happened?" he repeated, the anxiety in his voice clear.

"I received a threatening letter in my mail," she explained.

"I'll be right there," he said, and hung up.

Feeling safer knowing Paul was on the way and within the walls of her apartment, she laid the envelope on the dining table and tried to ignore its ugliness as she waited for Paul. She thought about calling Brody, but that would only upset him and bring him back to New York. If Paul thought she should call her brother, she would; otherwise, she'd let Paul do his job.

Twenty minutes later, Paul banged on her door. She couldn't contain the need to throw herself into his arms and for a moment his strong limbs closed around her, making her world seem that much safer. As she breathed in the spicy scent of his aftershave and could feel the rapid beat of his heart, she realized the barrier she'd crossed.

She'd initiated contact without any thought of germs or disease or anything that would have normally stopped her from reaching out. She slipped out of his embrace and stepped back to allow him to enter.

He peered at her, searching her face. "You okay?"

She nodded and pointed to the table. He produced rubber gloves from his inside coat pocket and slipped them over his hands. He carefully took the note out and read it. His gaze narrowed, his jaw hardening. "Do you have a big plastic bag?"

"Sure," she said, and hurried to the kitchen drawer where she kept them.

He took the offered bag and, using the tip of his finger, slipped the envelope inside. "I'll take this to the lab." He stripped off the rubber gloves. "Now will you listen to me and not place yourself in unnecessary danger?"

"Yes. Of course," she replied quickly, wondering if they both defined *unnecessary* danger the same. She had to be proactive. Everything she was doing was necessary.

"Good." He stared at her for a moment, his eyes unreadable. "I think I should go."

Suddenly she hated the thought of being alone. The killer obviously knew where she lived and was aware of her activities. "Can't you stay for a while?" she asked.

He held up the bag. "I need to have this processed."

Disappointment unfurled in her gut. "I see." She tried to understand. He had a job to do, she knew how that worked. But it didn't make her feel any better.

"I'll post a uniformed officer to stand watch outside your door. I'll come back by tomorrow," he said.

"I don't need a guard," she said, horrified at the idea. If she wanted someone stifling her movements, she'd call her brother. "I'll lock the door. I'll be fine."

The doubt in his eyes set her teeth together. "Look, really. The letter was a scare tactic. If someone wanted to hurt me, why send a warning?"

"I don't know, but I don't like leaving you alone."

She touched his arm. "If I get scared or anyone comes knocking, I'll call you."

At the threshold he hesitated. "Please be careful," he said.

"I will," she assured him.

Now that she was sure of the danger, she felt like she was balancing on a razor's edge with prison on one side and a murderer on the other.

Paul's gut churned with anxiety as he made his way to the crime lab, the bag containing the letter burning an imaginary hole in his pocket. The malicious threat meant someone was watching, keeping tabs on Megan's movements.

She was so stubborn and brave. And beautiful and quirky…and innocent. In so many ways. He couldn't believe how much she'd wiggled under his skin in the short time he'd known her. There were so many things he found appealing about her that drew Paul's thoughts repeatedly back to her.

He wasn't sure a future for them was possible, but for the first time in a long while he wanted to find out. But his priority was to catch a murderer.

He called Andy and asked to meet him at the crime lab. Twenty minutes later, after handing off the bag with the note, Paul and Andy headed to where Henry Vanderpool worked before his death.

The headquarters of the conglomeration of Fredrickson and Stiegel, an international financial service, was in the famed Chrysler Building. Once through the art deco décor of the lobby, they took the elevator to the fiftieth floor. To the right of the elevator, through a set of heavy, mahogany double doors, they entered the posh and stylized offices of Fredrickson and Stiegel.

The financial service's lobby was decorated in a festive Christmas motif, a small shimmering tree with wrapped presents beneath it taking up space near waiting chairs. Red-and-white stockings hung from gold ribbons tacked across the front desk. Paul recognized Handel's *Messiah* playing softly in the background.

Andy approached the very attractive brunette at the reception desk. He held out his badge for the woman's impassive inspection. "We're here about Mr. Vanderpool."

The woman's bright red lips turned down. "It's horrible what happened to him." She picked up her phone. "You'll want to talk with his assistant, Sally Heinen."

A few minutes later, an older woman in a well-tailored pantsuit glided toward them. Tall, slender, but not overly thin with dark graying hair pulled back into a slick bun, Sally Heinen held out her hand. "Detectives, what can I do for you?"

"We have some questions regarding Mr. Vanderpool," Paul said as he extracted his hand from her cold one.

"Please, let's talk in private." She turned on her high heels and motioned for them to follow. "This way, gentlemen."

She led them to a small conference room with a round table and six high-back leather captain's chairs. A pitcher of water and six glasses sat in the center of the dark wood table. "Gentlemen, please have a seat."

Paul complied, feeling as if he were visiting a law firm instead of an investment company. Sally Heinen exuded an aura of authority that made Paul wonder why she was an assistant and not in a position of higher power.

He took out his notepad. "Was Mr. Vanderpool at work the day of his murder?"

She inclined her head. "Yes."

Andy frowned. "Mrs. Vanderpool had stated he was supposed to be out of town."

Sally's thin, winged eyebrows rose. "Indeed."

"Did he have travel plans?" Paul asked.

Sally shook her head. "Not that I was aware of. In fact, we had meetings scheduled for the next few days, as several members of our parent company were coming in from Germany for the week. I don't know why Mrs. Vanderpool thought he was to be gone."

Andy sat forward, leaning his elbows on the table. "What was Mr. and Mrs. Vanderpool's relationship like?"

Sally gave a small smile. "That is a good question. I don't have an answer for you. Mrs. Vanderpool is not…" She took a breath in through her nose, her nostrils flaring slightly. "How to put this? She doesn't—didn't contribute to Mr. Vanderpool's business life."

"Meaning?" Paul probed.

"Meaning, we here at the office didn't see her often, except at the corporate functions that required her attendance. And even then, she would put in an appearance but leave quickly. I think Mrs. Vanderpool preferred to keep their private life, private."

The assistant was attractive. Was she involved with her boss? "The night of the murder, were you here with Mr. Vanderpool?"

"Yes. We worked until almost six preparing for the upcoming meetings," she said without hedging or coyness. "Then he received a phone call that must have been important because he packed up his briefcase and left."

"His briefcase?" Paul glanced at Andy. No briefcase had been found at the scene.

"It's here if you'd like to see it," Sally supplied. "Mr. Vanderpool apparently forgot it in the Town Car when he was dropped off at the gallery. The driver, Tony, brought it up the next day."

Andy said, "Yes, we definitely need to see that briefcase."

"And talk with the driver. We'll need his information." Paul made a note to talk with Tony. Maybe Vanderpool had mentioned who called him to the gallery. "Could you also supply us with the phone records of that night?"

She raised her chin. "Do you have a warrant?"

Paul met her gaze. "I can absolutely get one if need be. We have to know where the call that sent him to his death came from."

Sally blinked, her facing paling. "Well, of course. I can get that for you. All the calls come through the reception desk." She rose and left.

Paul rocked back in his chair. "So Mr. V wasn't supposed to be gone on business."

"Seems Mrs. Vanderpool has some explaining to do," Andy observed in a cynical tone.

Paul tapped his pencil against his notepad. "The pieces aren't adding up."

"No, they aren't," Andy agreed. "We have two

wives who've been cagey at best, who may or may not have motive, but means? Two gallery employees with questionable alibis, but means? Maybe, but motive?" He shrugged. "Can't put my finger on that. Then we have Megan McClain."

"She didn't do it," Paul stated forcefully.

Andy held up his hands. "I tend to agree with you. The evidence keeps pointing away from her."

Sally reentered the conference room, halting their discussion. She placed a printout on the table before Paul. With one well-manicured, white-tipped nail, she pointed to a highlighted number. "This is the call."

"Thank you." Paul took the page and folded it in half before rising from the chair. "You've been most cooperative."

Andy rose and pushed the chair back up to the table. "Do you know of anyone who'd want your boss killed?"

Sally shook her head. "No. Mr. Vanderpool may not have had the warmest of personalities, but he was a professional to a fault. He was a man who stood behind his word."

"One last question," Andy said before opening the door. "Did you ever hear Mr. Vanderpool mention a Megan McClain?"

She frowned. "No. I'd never heard of her until I read in the paper about her arrest."

"Did you know that Mr. Vanderpool had been in the market to purchase a piece of art from the Sinclair Gallery?"

Sally's mouth twisted. "Art was Mr. Vanderpool's passion. I know he bought several pieces through the Sinclair Gallery as well as others in town. Last summer he flew to France for an exhibit and brought home what he called his 'prize.' I believe he keeps it at his Long Island home."

"Thank you, Ms. Heinen." Paul handed her his business card before following Andy to the elevator. "If you think of anything that might be helpful, please, give us a call."

As Paul and Andy left the Chrysler Building, Andy suggested they go to Drake's office. "Let's see who his dinner was with and why he wasn't there."

Drake's law office was located on Williams off Wall Street. The tight, congested streets were hard to navigate. Andy finally dropped Paul off in front of the Duane Reade pharmacy across from Drake's building. Paul easily made his way through the slow-moving traffic on the one-way street and hurried beneath the scaffolding of another building getting a face-lift.

Inside the next building, he took the stairs to the second floor to a small office. Drake and Associates was stenciled in gold lettering on the etched-glass door.

Paul entered the small waiting area where several dark faux-suede chairs sat arranged around a coffee table littered with magazines. A water cooler gurgled in the corner. A single desk served as the reception area, protecting the door leading to what Paul assumed would be the associates' offices. A green wreath with a striped bow adorned the door.

A Hispanic woman with long, dark curly hair and heavily made-up eyes sat at the desk. She smiled in welcome. "Can I help you?"

Paul showed her his badge. "I'm investigating Mr. Drake's murder."

The young woman uttered a silent *Oh* and sat up straighter. She held up a finger and then dialed the phone. She turned her back as she spoke into the receiver. "There's a cop here wanting to talk about Mr. D."

She hung up, and said, "Please have a seat. Mr. Hargrove will be right with you."

Paul chose to stand near the water cooler. He figured Andy hadn't found a place to park so he'd be doing this solo. Within a few minutes a man opened the inner door and stepped into the reception area. He was tall with broad shoulders, dark blond hair and a chiseled face. He stared at Paul with a grim expression and put out his hand. "I'm Nigel Hargrove, Thomas's associate."

"Detective Wallace," Paul replied, and shook the man's hand.

"Come with me to my office," Nigel said, and led the way through a nicely appointed office space. Paul counted six individual offices, three on each side of the hall. At the end of the hall Nigel turned left into a corner office with large uncovered windows. The office directly across the hall, its door open, had a window, but a blind had been pulled down and the lights were off. Paul noticed the nameplate next to the open door. Thomas Drake.

Taking a seat in front of Nigel Hargrove's desk, Paul took out his notepad. "What can you tell me about Mr. Drake's last day?"

Nigel steepled his hands on his oak desk. "It was like any other. Busy. There are six associates here. Drake brought us together nearly twelve years ago now. His father-in-law fronted him the money to start the firm. We do mostly U.S. immigration law and nationality law. Thomas had a big case he was working on when he was killed."

"His wife has stated he was scheduled to be at a dinner meeting. Do you know who he was to have met?" Paul asked.

Nigel thought for a moment then shook his head. "No. But maybe his secretary, Lynn, would." He picked up the phone on his desk and punched in a number. "Lynn, could you come to my office, please. And bring Thomas's schedule with you."

Nigel hung up. "I read in the paper that you'd made an arrest. But you're here still investigating."

"Every bit of information is helpful," Paul stated politely.

"It's a real shame. I can only imagine how distraught Carol must be," Nigel said, his expression compassionate.

"Do you know Mrs. Drake well?" Paul asked, picturing the very tightly controlled woman he'd met.

"Not really. Christmas parties, that kind of thing. Thomas kept his home life separate from his office life."

The hairs on the back of Paul's neck rose. Hadn't Mr. Vanderpool's assistant said almost the exact thing? Two men who kept the two sides of their lives separate and private. That had to mean something.

"Ah, here's Lynn," Nigel said, his gaze over Paul's shoulder. "Come in."

Paul stood and turned to see a heavyset woman of about thirty standing hesitantly in the doorway. She had kind brown eyes and looked at Paul questioningly as she came forward. Nigel gestured for her to sit in the chair next to Paul. Paul resumed his seat as Nigel made the introductions.

"The detective here would like to see Thomas's schedule for the night of his murder." Nigel's voice hitched on the last word, obviously upset by his associate's demise.

Lynn's hands shook as she opened a leather-bound ledger. "There was nothing on his calendar for that day."

"He didn't have a business dinner?" Paul inquired.

Lynn shook her head, her short hair not moving. "Not that I knew of."

"Did you know about the painting he'd purchased the night before?" Paul asked.

Lynn nodded, her eyes sad. "Yes, it was to be a present for his wife's mother."

"Why didn't he have the painting delivered?" Paul wondered aloud. Why pick it up when it would have been more expedient to have the painting sent directly to his in-laws' or his own home?

Lynn cocked her head. "I wondered that, too."

Her eyes showed concern and compassion in their brown depths. She obviously cared for her boss. "Did you ever hear Mr. Drake mention Megan McClain?"

"No. Not that he would have discussed his girlfriends with me."

Paul raised his eyebrows. "Girlfriends?"

Lynn's gaze darted to Nigel and back to Paul as if not sure how to answer. "I don't want to speak ill of the dead, but Mr. Drake was a bit of a womanizer."

Whoa. Now that was an interesting lead that might get them somewhere. "Did his wife know?"

Nigel spoke up. "Thomas was discreet in his affairs. And he'd said he and Carol had an understanding."

"An understanding?" Paul sat back, trying to picture the scenario. Mrs. Drake hadn't seemed the type to stand for any impropriety. But first impressions were always deceiving. He'd thought Megan guilty the first time he'd laid eyes on her.

Nigel made a what-can-you-do gesture with his hands. "Thomas had an enormous appetite for life."

Paul scoffed. "Did you know that Drake abused his wife?" He threw the question out to see what reaction he'd get.

Lynn's eyes widened. "No, I didn't."

Nigel's lack of expression told Paul that the man had known.

"Mr. Hargrove?" Paul pressed.

Nigel sighed. "I'd heard rumors. I know Carol had been hospitalized a few times for supposed falls. But I never believed it. Thomas could be a hothead at times with an uncontrollable temper."

Enough to kill over a painting, only to have the deed somehow go bizarrely wrong? Paul turned his gaze to Lynn. "You never witnessed his temper?"

She bit her lip. "I've only been here for three months."

Paul turned back to Nigel, wanting to understand how the Drakes' lives had intersected. "Do you know how Mr. and Mrs. Drake met?"

"If I remember correctly, Thomas was in his first year of Harvard Law when he met Mr. Grieger, who took Thomas under his wing and introduced him to his only daughter, Carol. Carol, I believe, was attending Cornell. They waited until Carol graduated before they married."

"I see," Paul said. The story matched what Mrs. Drake had said. But why had she claimed he was at a business dinner?

Was she mistaken? Or had she lied?

Another thought occurred to him. Had Mr. Grieger realized his son-in-law was not treating his daughter well? If so, did he have something to do with the two murders?

Paul sighed with frustration. Because no matter how he looked at the events, he couldn't figure out how the missing painting ended up in Megan's apartment. What did Megan have to do with these two men?

ELEVEN

The next morning Megan arose earlier than normal, nervous and excited because Paul had called last night checking on her and also to ask if she was free for lunch. He said he had some questions to ask. She assumed questions to do with the murder investigation. She'd called her lawyer with the news of the letter, and Hillary had felt certain that the charges would be dropped now that there had been a threat.

To burn off her fear-induced excess energy, she jumped rope for an hour and then dragged out the small punching bag that her brothers had insisted she bring to New York so she could practice the street-fighting techniques she'd been forced to learn as a teen.

Patrick had been adamant that all of his younger siblings learn what their father had insisted he learn. Joseph McClain had wanted to make sure his children were able to defend themselves should it ever be necessary. Megan wondered if it was more because Patrick had been such a skinny bookworm as a teen that their father had started the tradition. And then Patrick continued it with her brothers and then her, much to their mother's chagrin.

Just as she had finished showering, her phone rang.

"Hello?"

"Hi, Megan. It's Paul."

She smiled and leaned against the wall. "Hi. How are you?"

"Good. Look, I'm going to have to reschedule our lunch."

Her shoulders sagged with disappointment. "Oh. Has something happened with the case?"

"I'm heading to Water Mill to question Mrs. Vanderpool," he replied in a lowered tone.

"Well, if I have to be blown off for lunch, that's a good enough reason," she quipped.

"I'm not blowing you off," came his offended reply.

"I'm joking," she said. "What you're doing is more important than lunch. Are we still on for Sunday, though?"

"Yes, definitely."

"Would you be willing to come to church with me on Sunday morning?" she asked, taking a chance he'd say yes.

There was a moment of silence before he replied. "I'll think about it."

"That's all I can ask," she said.

After they hung up, Megan sat at the dining table. She prayed for Paul and that new information would be revealed to bring the true criminal to justice. Only prayer didn't bring her the normal peace it usually did, and soon she grew restless.

She paced the living room until her gaze fell on the digital camera Ryan, her younger brother, had given to her for her last birthday.

Needing something to do, to take her mind off the lack of work and the fact that she was a murder suspect and a threat had been made against her life, she decided to take the camera and go outside. Maybe she could catch the person watching her on film.

She bundled up, using a hat and dark sunglasses to disguise herself, and with the camera in hand walked out into the late-morning brisk air.

As she walked along, she snapped off random shots, capturing the flavor of New York City's traffic with all lanes full and steam rising from the vents in the street. She caught a man kissing his girl on the corner beneath the street signs. Occasionally, she paused to turn around to see what, or rather who, was behind her. There were so many people going about their lives, it was hard to tell if anyone was specifically following or watching her. She kept moving.

On a hunch—Brody was always talking about how the McClain's were famous for their cop's hunches—she headed toward the park and toward the Mayfair Towers, taking pictures of the snow-covered bushes and white-dusted benches along the pathways. The sun peeked out through the clouds and sparkled off the frozen snow.

She veered away from entering too deeply into the park and stayed on the wide sidewalk of Fifth Avenue and cut across Fifty-ninth at the south end of the park. She captured several great images of the horse-drawn carriages, the horses adorned with red blankets and red ribbons, their hot breath showing in the cold air.

She kept walking and taking pictures until she stood across the street from the tall apartment building, not daring to go over to try to see Mrs. Drake again. She loitered for a few minutes, thinking she hadn't been blessed with any cop's hunch.

She was turning away when a black Lincoln Town Car came to a halt at the entrance to the towers and a lone figure walked out of the building, clad in a striking white fur. Megan held up the camera and zoomed in. Mrs. Drake. Megan sucked in a breath as she snapped off a shot before Mrs. Drake disappeared into the car.

Not wanting to miss this opportunity, Megan hailed a cab. She jumped in, giving instructions to the older driver to follow the Town Car in front of them. She sat back with a thunk as the taxi shot forward. *Paul would not like this,* she thought as she kept her gaze trained on the car ahead of her.

Megan's taxi followed the Town Car into Central Park and to Tavern on the Green. Megan snapped off photos of Mrs. Drake alighting from the car and heading into the famous restaurant. As soon as the other woman disappeared from view in the covered entrance, Megan paid the cab fare and jumped out before the several valets on hand could help her.

Slowly, she walked beneath the red awning toward the door, careful to keep from appearing as if she were stalking Mrs. Drake. She snapped off photos of the snow-dusted setting, marveling at how buffered by the city the restaurant felt because of the thick trees, bushes and uneven topography in this section of the park. The calliope of noises that she'd become so accustomed to faded into just the occasional honk of a horn in the distance.

One of the hosts, an average-height man, though charmingly distinguished in a splendidly cut three-piece suit, gave her a welcoming smile as she entered the restaurant. The narrow hall led to a room with tan stuccoed walls and dark exposed beams, giving off an old-world tavern feel.

"Do you have reservations?" the host asked, his gaze expectant.

Megan removed her sunglasses but left on her hat. Flustered, she smiled. "No." She held up her camera. "Can I just look?"

He inclined his head, and then turned to a young woman who appeared at his elbow. "Rochelle will take you on a tour."

"Perfect," Megan said as she followed the host-ess, her gaze moving over the guests, searching for Mrs. Drake.

In a soft voice, Rochelle explained the history of the tavern as she led Megan through the original structure to the glass-enclosed seating rooms. Megan forced herself to keep an eye out for her quarry while allowing herself to take in the beauty of the establishment and make the appropriate responses to her tour guide.

Megan's gaze snagged on a corner table. Mrs. Drake sat sipping from a crystal goblet. Next to her sat another woman whom Megan didn't recognize. Pretending to take photos of the hand-carved mirrors behind the women, she zoomed the camera and captured both women's faces.

Satisfied with her progress, she turned to her guide. "This has been lovely. Thank you so much."

Rochelle seemed surprised. "Do you want to see the upstairs?"

"I'm good. Just point to the way out."

"Right this way."

The host met her at the door. "Would you like a cab?"

"That would be wonderful." While she waited under the red awning, she scrolled through the images and studied the face of the woman with Mrs. Drake. There was something familiar about her but she couldn't place her.

Just as a taxi pulled up, Megan called Paul's cell phone.

"Where to, miss?" the driver asked.

She held up a finger to indicate she needed a moment as she waited for Paul to pick up.

"Wallace."

"Where are you?"

"Megan? Are you all right?"

The concern in his voice warmed her to her toes. "Yes. I'm fine. Where are you?"

"Sitting at my desk," he replied. "Has something happened? I'm coming over."

"No. I'll come to you."

"Megan, you shouldn't be out running around without someone with you."

She grimaced. "I've already left. I'll be there in a few minutes."

She hung up and then gave the cab driver the address of the Nineteenth Precinct and ignored the quiver of anxiety of how Paul would react when he found out what she'd done.

"You what?" Paul stared at Megan in disbelief.

She had the grace to look sheepish. "I followed Mrs. Drake."

He slapped his forehead with the palm of one hand. "No, no, no. That is so not okay. Did she see you?"

Little creases appeared between her eyebrows. "I don't think so. Besides, she wouldn't know what I look like."

"Did you not see your picture in the paper?" He couldn't believe how irresponsible she was with her life. Two men were murdered, she was being framed, she'd received a threatening letter and still she insisted on pulling crazy stunts like this.

Her frowned deepened. "No, I didn't see it. Besides, I wore my hat and sunglasses. My own mother wouldn't have recognized me." She waved away his concern. "She didn't see me. I'm sure. But look at these photos I took of her at lunch." She held up the camera with the back toward him so he could view the images.

"So she's having lunch with a friend. That's not a criminal activity."

"No, but I don't think I could go out in public looking so…so complacent if my husband had just been killed the week before," Megan stated with a huff.

No, he doubted she would. He had a feeling that when Megan loved, she loved with her whole heart. Mrs. Drake, on the other hand, had reasons not to be that mournful. "Let's see if one of the tech guys can blow these up."

With Megan close on his heels, he took the camera to the back offices where one of the computer experts was working at his desk. "Hey, Clyde, any chance you have time to download these pictures from this camera?"

Clyde adjusted his wire-rimmed glasses and sighed, then took the camera for inspection. After a moment, he said, "Sure. Will only take a second. Where do you want the pictures sent?"

"To my computer," Paul replied, aware of Megan standing so close that she brushed up against his shoulder and sent sensations ricocheting through his system.

In silence they watched Clyde extract cables from a box, hook up the camera to his computer and then with a few clicks, he was done. He handed the camera back. "There you go."

"Thanks. I owe you," Paul said, and guided Megan to his desk.

He quickly threw away the remains of his lunch and tidied up a bit before he realized what he was doing. Giving himself a shake, he sat and brought the pictures up full-screen.

Megan sat on the edge of his desk. "This other woman looks vaguely familiar."

Andy rose from his desk and came around to view the screen. "Who took these?"

Megan raised her hand halfway. "Me."

"Hey, what we got? Something of interest?" Maria Gonzales said as she joined the group. Then she frowned at the screen. "What are those two doing together?"

Paul swiveled around to face her. "What two?"

Maria pointed to the screen. "They are the widows Drake and Vanderpool."

"That's what's familiar. The eyes," Megan exclaimed. "Grace has her mother's eyes."

Paul exchanged a glance with Andy. Obviously, Mrs. Vanderpool had been avoiding their follow-up interview for a reason. He was glad Maria had recognized the widow. "Well, this is interesting."

Andy nodded. "Yes, the plot thickens." He scuffed Megan gently on the shoulder. "Good work."

Paul frowned. "Don't encourage her."

Megan grinned, looking like the cat that ate the canary.

"Let's get the widows in here and find out just what they are about," Paul stated. "And to think I felt a twinge of compassion at Mrs. Drake's 'parents never had time, sent me to boarding school' story."

"I'll get some uniforms on it right now," Andy said.

"They're probably still at the restaurant," Megan said. "They hadn't even been served their lunch when I left."

Andy saluted before moving purposely away toward the dispatch.

"So you think the two widows are in cahoots?" Megan asked.

"Could be. But the question remains, how did they get into the gallery?" Paul said aloud, his mind turning over the facts. Though Paul hated to admit it, Megan's amateur sleuthing may have paid off.

Maria tapped Paul on the shoulder and motioned with her head for some privacy. "I'll be right back," he told Megan, and followed Maria a few feet away. "What's up?"

She handed him a sheet of paper with an address. "The crime-scene tech is there now, but Sims called and said you might want to check the place out."

Not understanding, Paul asked, "What is this place?"

"Thomas Drake's love nest," Maria said, and then slid a glance toward Megan. "They found evidence of *her* there."

The news hit Paul in the solar plexus like the business end of a nightstick.

Had Megan been playing him all along?

Megan didn't understand what happened. One moment she was enjoying a pleasant camaraderie with Paul, and the next he was having her escorted out of the station house and to her apartment by a uniformed officer with instructions not to leave the premises.

Something that Maria had told him when she'd taken him aside had set him against her. But what?

He hadn't answered her questions before he blew out with Maria and Andy, leaving her with just the vague notion that she was somehow in trouble.

A feeling she was becoming increasingly familiar with.

She paced her apartment with restless agitation running rampant through her veins. She hated this helpless feeling. Her life was in other people's hands again.

A fleeting thought rebounded in her mind. What had Paul said? He'd felt a twinge of compassion for Mrs. Drake because she'd been shipped off to boarding school.

Just like Grace Vanderpool.

Just like Grace's mother, Sarah Vanderpool.

Megan opened her laptop and typed in the name of Grace's school, Covington's Academy. She searched through the school's Web site until she found what she wanted. The page listing alumni.

Carol Grieger's name was on the list. Since Megan didn't know Mrs. Vanderpool's maiden name, she searched the list for Sarah. There were three listed. One of them had to be the now Mrs. Vanderpool.

That was the connection. They had been friends at boarding school and now…now they had plotted together to kill their husbands?

But again it all came back to how they'd done it. How had they slipped into the gallery without Megan seeing them?

Paul had interviewed the other employees at the gallery and hadn't found cause to arrest anyone else.

But maybe with the knowledge that the two women had known each other for years, Paul would be able to get them to confess how they accomplished the murders and why they were trying to frame Megan.

Anger burned in her chest. She didn't know these two women. Why were they ruining her life?

She picked up the phone and called Paul's cell. The call went directly to voice mail.

"Paul, it's me. I found out something I think you should know. Mrs. Drake and Mrs. Vanderpool went to the same boarding school, Covington's Academy. They very well could have been friends for years. I hope that helps."

As soon as she pressed End, the phone rang. Her heart shimmered, thinking that Paul had seen she was calling and was calling back. "Paul?"

"Uh, no," came the female voice over the line. "Hi, Megan, this is Lacy."

Shaking off her disappointment, Megan said, "Hi, Lacy. What can I do for you?"

"I'm at the gallery warehouse and I think I discovered one of the paintings that went missing, but I'm not sure because I've never seen it before. But from the description you wrote in the ledger it could be the same one. I was hoping you could come take a look."

She hesitated. Paul had told her explicitly not to go anywhere. But he'd meant no more snooping on her own. Surely he wouldn't be mad if she went just down the street to the gallery. "I'll be right over."

"Thanks, I so appreciate it," Lacy said, relief evident in her voice.

Megan couldn't help the little burst of satisfaction in her gut. She'd known those paintings were there, but with the chaos that Lacy had created, it was little wonder that the works were misplaced.

Just before she entered the warehouse entrance at the side of the building, she tried Paul one more time. The voice mail picked up again.

"Paul, me again. I'm at the gallery. I'll try to call you later."

Pocketing the phone, she pushed through the entrance.

Paul held an empty prescription bottle with Megan McClain's name on the label in his latex-covered hand as something akin to betrayal snaked through his system. He told himself this bottle didn't prove she was Drake's girlfriend or that she was a murderer.

But how had the medicine ended up in the nightstand in Drake's love nest?

And the place had been wiped clean. Antibacterial wipes, the kind that Megan preferred, were found in the bathroom cupboard. A pink toothbrush, like the one he'd seen in Megan's bathroom in her apartment, now lay in an evidence bag.

This all seemed too staged. Megan had been free for a week; she would have retrieved her belongings if she were truly guilty.

"Detective," called Barbara Sims, the lead CSI tech. She held up a small square between her gloved fingers. "A micro SDHD card."

His eyebrows rose. "For a digital camera?"

Sims shrugged. "Or for a phone camera."

Paul hoped he wouldn't see pictures of Megan on that card. "Bag it and get it to Clyde ASAP."

There wasn't more for him to do here. He had to get to the station; he had two grieving widows to reinterview.

"Lacy?" Megan called out into the silent warehouse, a huge fifteen hundred by fifteen hundred space that at one time had been neatly organized and categorized. Now all around her gilded-frame works of art were stacked in varying degrees of sloppiness. Larger frames resting on smaller frames, some sideways, others even upside down. The need to fix the mess itched at Megan like a mosquito bite.

She heard a noise toward the far back corner.

Jamming her hands into her pockets to keep from righting a painting here or rearranging a painting there, Megan wound her way through the sea of art. When she reached where she thought the noise had come from, she found no one there. "Lacy?"

Irritated that Lacy would summon her and then leave without a note or anything, Megan turned back, intending to go into the gallery to find her when a sudden, sharp, blinding pain exploded in her lower back, sending her forward, her knees buckling, her hands instinctively coming up to break her fall.

The impact of hitting the floor stung her palms and bruised her knees, but the pain in her back took her breath away. She'd been stabbed. A whisper of movement to her right gave enough warning for her to roll to the left as something whooshed close to her head, scraping across the concrete floor, the metallic sound sparking terror in Megan's veins.

She scrambled backward, away from the wickedly pointed knife held in the leather-gloved grip of her assistant.

Lacy was trying to hurt her? Confusion and horror muddled her mind.

Her back hit a stack of paintings. She tried to brace herself enough to stand, but blood, dripping from the wound in her back, made the floor slick. She wiped her hand on her coat. The feel of her phone in her pocket gave her strength. Her mind told her to keep Lacy talking, keep her distracted.

"Lacy?" Megan asked. Disbelief echoed in the

quiet. Surreptitiously, she slid her hand into her pocket, her fingers fumbling with the phone. "What are you doing? Why are you hurting me?"

Lacy advanced; her blue eyes glittered in the low lighting like embers in a dying fire. "You should never have come to the gallery. I'm family. Me! Not you. But *no,* he gives my job to you. Tells me I'll learn from you, and then one day I could be as good as you."

Megan tried to wrap her mind around what the younger woman was saying as her fingers fumbled with which button was the send button. If she could only push Send, the phone would recall the last phone number dialed. Paul. "Lacy, I don't understand. I'm no longer a threat to you. You have my job."

Lacy scoffed. "Yeah, but I don't do it as well as the great Megan McClain. I'll never be as good as you. And he'd take you back in a heartbeat. But the gallery is mine. All mine now that he's gone."

Fear and dread lodged in Megan's throat. She tried to stay focused, but she knew she was losing a lot of blood from her back. "What did you do, Lacy? Where is Mr. Sinclair?"

Lacy laughed, an unbalanced sound that was absorbed by the canvases. She grinned and pointed the knife at Megan. "You killed him. You came here wanting your job back, and he wouldn't give it to you. So you killed him."

"And how will you explain my death?" Megan asked, pushing what she hoped was the right button on her phone. The tiny metallic ping sent her nerves ricocheting. She held her breath, waiting to see if Lacy noticed the noise. She didn't.

Please, God, make Paul hear, Megan pleaded silently as she fought to stay conscious.

"You two fought. He managed to get the knife in you before he expired." She grinned. "I have it all figured out. Just like last time."

Megan needed to keep Lacy talking, so Paul could hear what was going on. "Last time?"

Lacy moved closer. "My lover, Thomas, wouldn't divorce his wife, no matter how much I begged or how much he professed to love me. So I went to her thinking she'd divorce him, but no, she couldn't, she said. Something about a prenuptial agreement." Lacy waved her hand. "But then she comes up with this idea. And it would have worked if that other man hadn't shown up." She frowned. "I still don't get why he was there."

Horror unraveled through Megan. "So you killed Mr. Drake *and* Mr. Vanderpool."

Lacy frowned. "Yes. Only, that other guy wasn't supposed to be there. *You* were."

Megan swallowed hard as understanding washed away the last of her naiveté. Mrs. Vanderpool must have told her husband to go to the gallery. "Do you know Mrs. Drake and Mrs. Vanderpool are friends?"

Lacy's gaze narrowed. "What?"

"They manipulated you to kill both of their husbands," Megan said as the pieces came together. "And you tried to frame me for the murders."

Lacy's mouth twisted. "Yeah, well, I'll do a better job this time."

Terror squeezed Megan's lungs. She didn't want to die. She didn't want to leave her family, couldn't bear the thought of them grieving for her. She didn't want to leave Paul when they'd just found each other. She wanted time to see where a relationship could go with him. She wanted to explore the world with the strength and knowledge she'd learned from Paul. She wanted time to conquer her fears and master her illness.

She had to take control of the situation if she wanted to live. She forced her feet under her and, gripping the edge of the Warhol painting at her back, she managed to stand. She swayed, the room spun. "You won't get away with this, Lacy. I won't let you kill me."

Lacy raised the knife. "Yes, I will. And yes, you will, because you're weak, Megan. You can't even stand up to a tiny little germ."

Bracing her feet apart, Megan tightened her hold on a gilded frame, elevating it an inch off the ground. As Lacy rushed forward ready to drive home the knife into Megan's chest, Megan lifted and swung the frame, catching Lacy in the face. The knife clattered to the ground. Lacy fell sideways and landed unconscious in a heap.

Megan kicked the knife far away and sank to the floor as the rush of adrenaline that had been compensating for her blood loss seeped away.

As the world faded to a pinprick of light, she whispered, "I'm not in control. Only You are, God. Please, watch over Paul."

TWELVE

As soon as Paul and Andy were in the sedan headed back uptown, Paul's phone rang.

"Wallace."

"Hey, I've been trying to get you for the past half hour on your cell as well as the car radio," Maria said, with a hint of censure.

"No signal," Paul replied. "We just got back in the car."

"We have your two widows in custody. They've both asked for their lawyers." Maria sounded pleased with herself.

"Great," Paul quipped with derision. "We'll just have us a party."

"What's up?" Andy asked as Paul hung up.

"The widows have lawyered up. We won't get anywhere with them tonight." His phone buzzed before he could even get it back in his coat pocket. But it was simply letting him know he had five missed calls. Two from the station and three from Megan. He punched in his voice-mail code. He listened to the first message.

"Hey, Megan discovered the two ladies went to the same boarding school," he informed Andy, impressed that she'd come up with such useful information.

"She's a regular Nancy Drew, isn't she?" Andy replied with approval in his tone.

"Yeah." Paul continued to listen to the recorded messages. The second two messages were from Maria. He frowned as he heard Megan's second message saying she was heading over to the gallery. Frustration ticked in his jaw. He'd told her to stay put at home. When Megan's third message played, at first it was all garbled, but then he heard voices. Megan's. And another woman's.

His heart froze with terror as the impact of what he was hearing hit him like a sledgehammer to the chest.

Megan needed him.

Paul burst through the front door of the gallery, Andy hot on his heels. "Where's Megan?"

Joanie blinked, her big brown eyes wide. "I haven't seen her. What's wrong?"

"Where's Lacy? And Sinclair?" Paul barked, his gaze frantically searching for Megan as he stormed toward the office stairs. If anything happened to Megan, he wouldn't be able to live with himself.

"They're not upstairs. They're in the warehouse," Joanie replied, chasing after him.

"How do we get there?" Andy asked, in a calm but urgent tone as he rushed out of the workroom where he'd gone in search of Megan.

"Around the side of the building. There's a set of steel double doors," Joanie said, her face ashen. "You'll need the access code."

Paul ran back outside, slipping on the slush-covered sidewalk, his heart constricting in his chest. He skidded to a halt at the double doors and waited impatiently for Joanie to punch in the security code on the square pad by the door. An audible click sounded and Paul yanked open the door, barely registering Andy's help.

"Megan!" he bellowed as he charged forward into the gloomy warehouse. Paintings of all sizes and shapes littered every available space. Shelves lined one wall, its sculptured artifacts looking haphazardly placed. The warehouse looked more like a junk room than a cataloged inventory. Megan wouldn't have allowed such chaos to reign.

A groan brought his attention to the back of the building. He darted forward, uncaring that he dislodged stacked paintings in his wake. His heart leaped to his throat and choked him when he caught sight of Megan's limp body. Blood was pooled around her, a dark crimson stain on the concrete floor. A few paces away, Lacy Knight was just coming to. She must have been the one who'd groaned. Paul's vision narrowed.

"You deal with her," Paul bit out to Andy as he dropped to his knees to check Megan's pulse. Thready, but there. The thin ribbon of relief did nothing to dispel the horror he felt. In self-defense, he went into battlefield mode, stifling his own emotions as best he could.

He smoothed back her hair from her forehead. "You'll be okay. Hang in there, honey." But nothing he'd ever experienced in any war zone had prepared him for the prospect of losing the woman he loved. "I can't lose you," he whispered as tears clogged his throat.

The wail of a siren filled the warehouse, and soon Paul was pushed aside so the EMTs could attend to Megan. Their assessment was grim, and they wasted no time getting her to the hospital. She'd lost a lot of blood from the knife wound in her back.

Paul's heart squeezed tight, robbing him of breath as he watched the ambulance disappear down the street. "Please, God. Please, don't take her from me. I love her."

Four long hours, Paul paced the waiting area of the county emergency room as the E.R. doctors worked to save Megan's life. Every time the door to the E.R. swung open he held his breath, expecting the doctor or nurse to give him some news.

But so far no one had come to tell him how Megan was doing.

Her family was on the way. Paul had called as soon as he'd been able to leave the crime scene.

Andy came rushing through the outside doors, his cashmere overcoat flapping behind him like wings. "Have you heard anything?"

Paul shook his head and rubbed at his gritty eyes. "No. Nothing."

Andy laid a hand on Paul's shoulder. "She'll pull through. She's a strong woman."

Paul could only pray that was true.

"Detective?" called a woman in green scrubs as she came through the swinging emergency-room doors.

"Yes. Megan McClain?" Tension coiled in Paul's veins.

The woman gave him a reassuring smile. "She's holding her own. Thankfully, the knife didn't hit any vital organs. She did lose an awful lot of blood, though. We've given her a transfusion. Now, we have to wait and see what her body will do. We have to take it moment by moment, one step at a time."

Tears burned the back of Paul's eyes. Moment by moment, one step at a time. That was so Megan.

"Her prognosis is good," a kind voice said somewhere over Megan's head.

"That's…that's wonderful," came another voice, a voice Megan recognized. *Paul.*

She struggled toward him through the murky depths of darkness that resisted her attempts at cognitive thinking. She needed to see him, to warn him of the danger. She had to get to him.

Slowly, she managed to emerge to the light, her eyes cracking open, her gaze searching until she saw him, his face haggard and unshaven, his eyes bloodshot and tired.

He noticed her stare and smiled. "Doctor, she's coming around."

"So she is," that other voice said, and then her eyelids were being pulled open, and a light shone in. She shrank away, wanting only to see Paul.

He took her hand, the warmth curling like ribbon over her and tying her heart up in a pretty bow. "You're okay, Megan," Paul said. "You're in the hospital. Your family is on their way."

Hospital? "Lacy!" she tried to say, her voice weak as fear gripped her.

"She's in jail. As are Mrs. Drake and Mrs. Vanderpool. You don't have to be afraid any longer. You're safe."

"Mr. Sinclair?" She hated to think what Lacy had done to him.

"He's in ICU, but he's going to make it."

Relief swept over her in a wave and tried to take her back to the darkness. She fought it, forcing her eyes open to stare into the face of man she loved.

Her breath caught. She loved Paul. She searched her heart and found that as truth.

She had to tell him, now before she lost her nerve.

"Paul, listen to me," she said, her voice shaky with emotion. "I have so much to be thankful for. You especially. I tried so hard for so long to overcome my OCD on my own but your belief in me, that has made a world of difference. Knowing that you believed in me gave me strength to conquer my fears. And gave me the courage to seek out the truth." She grimaced. "I know I tried to be in control of everything, but only God is in control. I've realized that."

She clutched his hand, feeling like her heart was flayed open for him to see. "I want you to know how much I've come to love you." She swallowed hard and forced herself to continue even in the face of his stunned expression. "I do. I love you. And I know you don't love me. But maybe, someday. Someday we could meet again. And it could be for the first time. I just know I want to have a chance."

Paul swiped his free hand through his hair. "Megan, I don't know what to say."

"You don't have to say anything," she said as tears crested her lashes.

Before she had a chance to really understand the ramifications of her declaration, her family descended. Deep voices filled the room, three big men jostling to get closer. Paul released her hand, and she whimpered.

Then her gaze took in her brothers. Patrick, the academic, in his tweed, with his warm brown eyes searching her face behind his glasses. Then Brody, muscled and solid, worry lines bracketing his mouth and dark eyes. And finally Ryan, her baby brother, as dashing as ever in a Hawaiian-print shirt, his usually dancing eyes anxious.

Her heart swelled with love for her brothers, even as her heart ached for what Paul hadn't said, that he cared for her.

Then her mother squeezed through to take the forefront position, and Megan had never been happier to see the fierce protective love in her mother's eyes than at that moment. More tears gathered in

Megan's eyes and slipped down her cheeks as her mother moved in for a gentle hug. Megan breathed in deeply her mother's floral scent that soothed her soul. In her peripheral vision, she saw Brody shake hands with Paul, before Paul walked out of the hospital room.

And out of her life.

Paul stared out the one window in his small one-bedroom Gramercy Park apartment. Outside, the world seemed the same, everyone going about their lives, preparing for the Christmas celebration, but for Paul the world had been changed.

Changed by words so honest and touching, so like Megan herself.

He couldn't believe the depth of emotion she confessed to nor the way his heart responded. He'd been so stunned—he hadn't been able to find words. Words to tell her of the depth of his own feelings. And then the moment passed and her family was there, crowding in to see her. He'd felt like an intruder, so he'd left. That was a week ago.

The four walls of the apartment closed in on him, making him restless. The need to move overcame him. Pacing didn't help. He stared at the posters lining the walls of his apartment. Baseball's greats, athletes who had inspired him to dream as a child.

But did he have the courage to dream of a life with Megan?

His gaze drifted to the Medal of Valor displayed

in a shadow box on the bookshelf, given to him for courageous service to his country.

Pivoting, he retraced his steps across the old worn carpet, his gaze snagging on his badge, the hunk of shiny brass twinkling in the lamplight representing bravery, justice and truth. Things he'd fought for since the day he'd entered the academy.

But was he willing, did he have the courage to fight for a future with Megan?

Her words came back to him, *Knowing that you believed in me gave me strength to conquer my fears.*

Knowing she loved him, he had the courage to fight for what he wanted. Her.

He glanced at the clock on the kitchen wall. It was too late to call her on Christmas Eve.

He longed to hear her voice. To see her. To assure himself that her words weren't a medicinally induced litany, but rather words of hope for a future together.

He had to see her. He should wait until after the holiday. He really should. But he couldn't wait.

If he caught the morning train, he'd be in Boston by midmorning. In a flurry, he packed and left his apartment at the crack of dawn, armed with a heart full of hope.

Christmas morning arrived with lots of love, snow and laughter in the McClain household. A beautiful Christmas tree winked in the corner of the living room, throwing a kaleidoscope of color on those gathered around. Spent wrapping paper littered every unused space, and gifts were piled all over.

Megan had been released from the hospital to her mother's care while her wound healed. Only her heart hurt more than the cut in her lower back. There had been no contact with Paul since the hospital a week ago.

From her place in the recliner, Megan watched the generous affection of her brothers with their wives, or soon-to-be wife, in Ryan's case.

Brody and Kate shared the overstuffed chair by the fireplace with baby Joseph bouncing on Brody's knee. She marveled that Brody had a son and her heart melted to see her big, strong brother reduced to cooing and giggling.

Patrick and Anne sat on the floor at the foot of the couch holding hands and looking so comfortable together. Megan was so proud of her eldest brother for having fought to stay with Anne during her days in the witness protection program.

Ryan and his exotic beauty, Kiki, sat on the couch, Ryan's arm slung casually over Kiki as she leaned into his chest. They hadn't planned to come to Boston until closer to Patrick and Anne's renewing of their vows on New Year's Day, but when Ryan had heard that his big sister was hurt, he and Kiki had immediately flown to Boston. Megan's heart swelled with love at their sacrifice of leaving their island over the Christmas holiday.

With a flourish, Colleen McClain entered the room carrying a tray with their traditional Christmas morning Irish cake, a solid and heavy mixture of fruits and spices prepared months in advanced and iced with marzipan right before serving. The recipe had been handed down from generation to generation in her mother's Irish family.

Memories of Christmas mornings past flooded Megan, filling her with nostalgia and a twinge of sadness. She'd always missed her father most at Christmas.

She and her brothers exchanged glances of warmth and love as her mother sat the cake on the coffee table.

Everyone quieted down for their mother's Irish blessing. Before she could speak, there was a knock at the door.

"I'll get it," Brody said, handing Joseph to Kate and getting up.

A moment later he reappeared, his gaze zeroed in on Megan.

He looked a bit stunned as he said, "You have a visitor."

He stepped aside to reveal Paul. Megan's breath hitched and caught. She drank in the sight of him. He wore jeans and his leather bomber jacket. His sandy hair was damp from the snow and his gaze uncertain.

"I'm sorry to impose," he said, never looking away from her.

She blinked as questions bombarded her. Had something gone wrong with the case? Was she once again a suspect? Or was he here for her? A flush of embarrassment worked its way up her neck as she recalled the way she'd bared her soul to him the last time she'd seen him.

Colleen moved to pull Paul farther into the room. "Come in, come in. Please join us. I was about to give the blessing before breakfast."

Brody brought a dining-room chair in and sat it next to Megan. She smiled at him gratefully as the butterflies trapped in her stomach tried to get out.

Paul sat down, his green-eyed gaze searching hers.

Megan couldn't take her eyes off Paul as her mother's voice, falling back on the soft brogue of her youth, filled the room.

"May the light of the Christmas star be upon you. The warmth of home and hearth be yours. The cheer and goodwill of friends to you each. With the hope of a childlike heart. And may the joy of a thousand angels caress you. Let the love of the Son, and God's peace, fill you all, my darlings."

For a moment her words hung in the air, a prayer of love, before she clapped her hands in her very motherly way. "All right now. I think this young man needs a moment alone with Meggie. We'll cut the cake in the kitchen. Come along everyone."

Colleen shooed the family out of the living room, but when she turned to leave, she met Megan's gaze. Megan read the love and worry in her mother's blue eyes. Megan gave her mother a nod of reassurance. She would be safe with Paul.

When they were alone, Paul took her hand. "I had to see you."

Pleased by his statement, she said, "So you came here."

He nodded. "I told myself to wait until after Christmas." His mouth quirked. "But you know life isn't tidy and sensible, so I came to see you on Christmas morning."

Joy filled her chest. "I'm glad you did."

He smiled and tucked a piece of her hair behind her ear, his touch lingering on her face. "I couldn't let another day go by without you knowing."

Her mouth went dry. "Knowing what?"

"That I love you."

She saw it there in the depths of his eyes and her heart soared, but she held tight to the tether of her old life. She had to tell him one last thing. "I have obsessive-compulsive disorder," she stated flatly, fully prepared to see the withdrawal and the pity in his eyes that usually came whenever anyone found out.

His gaze softened to a tender caress. "I know. You told me. It doesn't matter. I love you, quirkiness and all."

She let loose the tether and beamed at him as her heart took flight.

EPILOGUE

Eighteen months later; Maui, Hawaii

A trade wind kicked up, swirling the floral-scented air through the wedding guests and making the fragrant fields of flowers sway merrily. Megan took a moment to savor the tropical scents and the sounds of the distant ocean crashing against the cliffs. Some unseen exotic bird squawked from one of the many hala trees dotting the hillside surrounding the Kapaa Flowers Bed-and-Breakfast located on a prime piece of real estate on the island of Maui.

Her brothers and two of Kiki's male cousins stood on the steps of the pretty gazebo at one end of the lush stretch of manicured lawn. All five men looked heartbreakingly handsome in their black tuxes, waiting for the wedding march to play that would send the bride and her bridesmaids to the waiting men. The pastor, a man Megan couldn't quite tell the nationality of—a mix of African-American and

Asian—stood in the center of the gazebo with his Bible in his hands.

From where Megan stood waiting to walk in the wedding procession at the back of the focal point of the bed-and-breakfast—a new, large craftsman-style house—Megan's gaze searched the crowd of wedding guests for Paul. She spotted him off to the side talking with a big Hawaiian man, Nik something, whom she'd met earlier in the day.

Paul was the most handsome of them all in a light beige suit, which she imagined he was on the brink of shedding half of even though the morning heat of the sun hadn't really hit its peak. Already he'd loosened the elegant tie and unbuttoned his coat. She certainly couldn't blame him. Her own floral dress was already sticking to her skin.

The red-haired wedding planner that Kiki had hired to orchestrate her wedding to Ryan said, "Okay, ladies, here we go." She moved their line like a drill sergeant. "Kiki, veil down."

Megan smiled while watching how Colleen McClain, Kiki's mother and grandmother all vied for the opportunity to fuss over Kiki. Dear Kiki took their help in stride as she prepared to walk down the aisle on the arm of her father. Mr. Brill, tall and distinguished in his own formal wear, waited patiently with a bemused smile on his face.

"Moms and grandmoms, your escorts." The red-haired planner hustled the women to the men waiting to escort them to their seats.

"You're next to get married, you know," whispered Anne from her place beside Megan. She, too, wore the pretty floral frock that Kiki had provided for her three soon-to-be sisters-in-law and her cousin, Amber, a spirited young woman who bounced on her toes as if ready to sprint to life's finish line.

Megan smiled with longing. She sure hoped so. Paul hadn't asked her yet, but their relationship had been growing stronger with each passing day.

"Here we go, the youngest McClain about to tie the knot," Kate said as she joined them on the steps as Kiki and her father moved forward.

"All right, ladies," the planner said. "Quiet now." She turned to the pianist and gave a nod.

The wedding march lifted into the air and the procession started forward. Amber first, then Kate, Anne and Megan. Kiki and her father followed.

During the ceremony, Megan marveled at how much she'd grown as a person since that fateful December night. She'd learned control was an illusion and that trusting in God was the only security she needed. She'd become less anxious and more adventurous. She'd also become less isolated and was continually making friends. Mr. Sinclair had rehired her once she was well enough to return to her own apartment and work. She'd hired a new assistant at the gallery and a friendship was blossoming. Megan had deepened her friendship with Joanie and formed a bond with Paul's family.

But the most important change was her relationship with Paul.

Her gaze strayed dreamily to him and for the rest of the ceremony their gazes held, his eyes full of gentleness and promises she longed to explore.

When the pastor introduced Ryan and Kiki as husband and wife, a sharp yearning to one day be Mrs. Paul Wallace filled Megan. She wanted her own happily-ever-after, like her brothers and their wives.

But God knew her heart, and if she and Paul were meant to marry, it would happen. She forced her mind back to the wedding procession as she followed the newly married McClain back down the aisle.

Later, with the reception in full swing, Megan found herself alone; her brothers had dragged Paul away for some male bonding and her sisters-in-law were mingling with the local guests. Megan wandered away from the cheery crowd toward the cliffs overlooking the Pacific Ocean.

The intense blues and greens seemed almost surreal against the cloudless, paler blue sky. Off in the distance a sailboat drifted on the horizon.

"Megan, are you okay?"

She turned at the sound of Paul's concerned voice and smiled softly when he stopped beside her. He'd taken off his jacket, lost his tie and rolled up the cuffs of his dress shirt. He looked far more comfortable and straight out of her dreams.

"Yes. I'm great. I can see why Ryan decided to move here."

Paul took her hand. A delicious shudder heated her from the inside out at the impact of his gentle grip.

"It's very intoxicating, all this fresh air and exotic setting. Makes me think anything is possible," he said, his voice low and intriguing.

"What do you mean?" she asked, searching his face.

Sunlight reflected off his honey-blond hair and his green eyes danced. From the pocket of his slacks, he pulled out a small square box and then slowly opened the lid to reveal a square-cut diamond solitaire on a circle of platinum.

Megan's breath stalled, her gaze mesmerized by the twinkling stone. Then she lifted her gaze, questioning the meaning, not daring to assume a thing for fear of being disappointed. The confirmation she saw in his eyes caused joy to bubble from within her until it burst forth in a laugh of delight.

"I take it you like?" Paul asked, his voice full of emotion.

"I like."

He took the ring out of the box, then shoved the box back in his pocket before taking her hand. He poised the diamond ring at the tip of her finger. "Megan, will you marry me?"

Choked with tears of happiness, she nodded.

He slipped the ring on her finger. It fit perfectly.

Pulling her into his embrace, Paul said, "Thank you. Thank you, thank you, thank you."

She leaned back to stare at him in wonder. "Why are you thanking me?"

"Because you are making me the happiest man alive," he said, and kissed her.

Suddenly afraid, she pulled away. "No, what I'm doing is saddling you with an obsessive-compuls—"

He stopped her with a gentle finger to her lips. "Megan, God sent you to me to save me from my jaded, hopeless self. He sent you to show me what I'd see if I stopped looking for evil long enough to see what good looked like. You reminded me there's beauty in this world. And how much strength and honor can be found in simply putting one foot in front of the other. I want to spend my life being worthy of you."

His words infused her with a peace she'd never imagined she'd feel. Blissful contentment filled her heart. "I truly don't think that's going to be a problem, Detective. I truly don't."

* * * * *

Dear Reader,

Thank you for reading *Double Threat Christmas*. I hope you enjoyed the last book of the McClain family. Megan and Paul had to learn that God is always in control and no matter how much we try to orchestrate our lives, we can't do as good a job as God can in giving us everything we need.

I will miss the McClain clan and all their adventures amid murder, mayhem and mystery. If Megan's story is your first introduction to THE McCLAINS, you'll want to find Brody's story in *Double Deception*, Patrick's story in *Double Jeopardy* and Ryan's story in *Double Cross*.

Blessings,

DISCUSSION QUESTIONS

1. What made you pick up this book to read? Did it live up to your expectations?

2. Did you think Megan and Paul were realistic characters? Did their romance build believably?

3. Talk about the secondary characters. What did you like or dislike about the people in the story?

4. Was the setting clear and appealing? Could you "see" where the story took place?

5. For Megan, she so wanted to be in control of her life. How did this need for control affect her choices? Do you think we can control our circumstances? Why or why not?

6. Paul's goal to find out the truth meant he had to go with his instincts. Have you ever had to rely on instinct? Where does instinct come from? Do you believe that God talks to us?

7. Did the suspense element of the story keep you guessing? Why or why not?

8. Did you notice the scripture in the beginning of the book? What application does it have to your life?

9. Did the author's use of language/writing style make this an enjoyable read? Would you read more from this author?

10. What will be your most vivid memories of this book?

11. What lessons about life, love and faith did you learn from this story?

Love Inspired

Determined to keep his sister from eloping, Cade Porter hires wedding planner Sara Woodward to arrange the wedding. She might be the best in the state, but she still finds Cade incredibly arrogant. After all, shouldn't his sister have a say in the most important day of her life? Not to worry, Cade assures the lovely Sara… she can plan *their* wedding right down to the day!

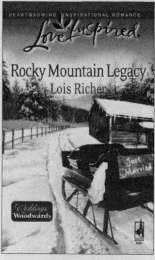

Look for

Rocky Mountain Legacy

by

Lois Richer

Weddings by Woodwards

Available January wherever books are sold.

www.SteepleHill.com

Steeple Hill®

LI87511

Love Inspired.
HISTORICAL
INSPIRATIONAL HISTORICAL ROMANCE

Working as a respectable
schoolteacher is the
one second chance
Annie MacAllister never
expected. Even more
surprising is that she
finds herself actually
helping her students—
not to mention Trail
End's most intriguing
citizen, John Sullivan.
Together they will need
divine forgiveness to
reignite their faith…and
find a future together.

Look for

Second Chance Bride
by
JANE MYERS PERRINE

*Available January
wherever books are sold.*

Steeple
Hill®

www.SteepleHill.com

LIH82803

REQUEST YOUR FREE BOOKS!

2 FREE RIVETING INSPIRATIONAL NOVELS
PLUS 2 FREE MYSTERY GIFTS

YES! Please send me 2 FREE Love Inspired® Suspense novels and my 2 FREE mystery gifts (gifts are worth about $10). After receiving them, if I don't wish to receive any more books, I can return the shipping statement marked "cancel". If I don't cancel, I will receive 4 brand-new novels every month and be billed just $4.24 per book in the U.S. or $4.74 per book in Canada, plus 25¢ shipping and handling per book and applicable taxes, if any*. That's a savings of over 20% off the cover price! I understand that accepting the 2 free books and gifts places me under no obligation to buy anything. I can always return a shipment and cancel at any time. Even if I never buy another book, the two free books and gifts are mine to keep forever.

123 IDN ERXX   323 IDN ERXM

Name _____ (PLEASE PRINT)

Address _____ Apt. #

City _____ State/Prov. _____ Zip/Postal Code

Signature (if under 18, a parent or guardian must sign)

Order online at www.LoveInspiredSuspense.com
Or mail to Steeple Hill Reader Service:

IN U.S.A.: P.O. Box 1867, Buffalo, NY 14240-1867
IN CANADA: P.O. Box 609, Fort Erie, Ontario L2A 5X3

Not valid to current subscribers of Love Inspired Suspense books.

Want to try two free books from another series?
Call 1-800-873-8635 or visit www.morefreebooks.com

* Terms and prices subject to change without notice. N.Y. residents add applicable sales tax. Canadian residents will be charged applicable provincial taxes and GST. Offer not valid in Quebec. This offer is limited to one order per household. All orders subject to approval. Credit or debit balances in a customer's account(s) may be offset by any other outstanding balance owed by or to the customer. Please allow 4 to 6 weeks for delivery. Offer available while quantities last.

Your Privacy: Steeple Hill Books is committed to protecting your privacy. Our Privacy Policy is available online at www.SteepleHill.com or upon request from the Reader Service. From time to time we make our lists of customers available to reputable third parties who may have a product or service of interest to you. If you would prefer we not share your name and address, please check here. ☐

LISUS08R

A SECRET PAST, A PRESENT DANGER...

HANNAH ALEXANDER

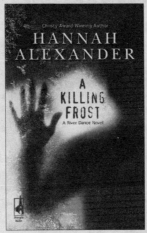

A terrible secret haunts Dr. Jama Keith. But she must return to her past—her hometown of River Dance, Missouri—and risk exposure. She owes a debt to the town for financing her dreams. If only she can avoid old flame Tyrell Mercer—but River Dance is too small for that.

When Tyrell's niece is abducted by two of the FBI's most wanted, Jama can't refuse to help—Tyrell's family were like kin to her for many years. The search for young Doriann could cost Tyrell and Jama their lives. But revealing her secret shame to the man she loves scares Jama more than the approaching danger....

A KILLING FROST

Available wherever trade paperbacks are sold!

Steeple
Hill®

Love Inspired®
SUSPENSE

TITLES AVAILABLE NEXT MONTH

Don't miss these four stories in January

HEART OF THE NIGHT by Lenora Worth
When secret agent Eli Trudeau discovers his son is alive,
he's furious with Gena Malone, the boy's adoptive mother.
Yet even his anger can't blind him to Gena's love for the
boy. And when someone dangerous comes after them,
Eli will do *anything* to protect his newfound family.

WHAT SARAH SAW by Margaret Daley
Without a Trace

The three-year-old witness is FBI agent Sam Pierce's
best resource when the girl's mother vanishes. Yet child
psychologist Jocelyn Gold will barely let him near Sarah.
Or herself. But for the child's sake—and her mother's—
Sam and Jocelyn must join forces to uncover just what
Sarah saw.

BAYOU BETRAYAL by Robin Caroll
Monique Harris has found her father—in prison
for murder. Still, when Monique is suddenly widowed,
she seeks refuge in the bayou town of Lagniappe, not
knowing *someone* doesn't want her to stay. Deputy sheriff
Gary Anderson has Monique hoping for a new future...
if she can lay the past to rest.

FLASHOVER by Dana Mentink
Firefighter Ivy Beria is frustrated when she's injured on the
job...until she realizes the fire was no accident. The danger
builds when her neighbor disappears. With the help of
friend and colleague Tim Carnelli, Ivy starts searching for
answers, but she might find something more—like love.

LISCNM1208BPA